BLOOD IN A DRY TOWN

A TENNY MATEO MYSTERY

E.B. WHEELER

Rowan Ridge
Press

OTHER BOOKS BY E.B. WHEELER

British Historical Fiction:

The Haunting of Springett Hall

Born to Treason

The Royalist's Daughter

Wishwood

Moon Hollow

Utah Historical Fiction

No Peace with the Dawn (with Jeffery Bateman)

Bootleggers and Basil (in *The Pathways to the Heart*)

Letters from the Homefront

The Bone Map

Utah Women: Pioneers, Poets, and Politicians

Print ISBN: 978-1-7321631-9-5

First printing: June 2020

Published by Rowan Ridge Press, Utah

Cover and interior design © Rowan Ridge Press

Front cover photos © Kenneth Keifer; nightowl

❀ Created with Vellum

To my grandmother, Corris Cram Brooksby,
for sharing her stories of southern Utah

CHAPTER ONE

Tarantulas. Scorpions. Snakes. The darkness of a root cellar had offered plenty of things for me to fear when I was a child. But now, standing on the red dirt ramp leading underground, the thing that made my fingers clammy on the cold metal of my Beacon flashlight was ghosts. Serving with the Red Cross in the trenches of the Western Front had taught me what lurked beyond the edges of the light.

Southern Utah was my haven, though. Here at home once again, the juniper-studded canyons, jagged red cliffs, and sandy dirt roads kept the outside world's problems far away. And the nastiest scorpions lived south of the Grand Canyon, so nothing to fear. There were no dead soldiers heaped on the floor of Mother's root cellar.

Only the ghosts I had brought back with me.

I gripped the fabric of my skirt and took a few more steps down. The flashlight cast a long, pale beam into the cave-like darkness. A couple more feet, and I would be able to see the bins of potatoes and the Mason jars of canned fruit. Already, the damp coolness of the earth rose around me to sap the warmth from the desert sun. And the shadows were inky black, waiting for the light to falter.

Don't look at the darkness. Focus on the flashlight beam and move forward with it.

But there's something universal about the smell of underground, whether in Utah or in France. Dank, earthy, almost metallic beneath that. It's easy to imagine a hint of blood in the mix.

No, it's just a root cellar.

I took another step. Almost there. This time, I would conquer the darkness.

A low buzz rose over the distant lowing of cattle. The building thrum vibrated in my chest. An airplane. I hadn't seen or heard one since the Great War ended a year and a half ago. I scanned the cloudless blue expanse still visible behind me.

A Curtiss Jenny biplane dipped over the sagebrush-studded pastures, its tail painted red, white, and blue, and the number 976 in black on the fabric stretched over its spruce wood frame. The fast *chop-chop-chop* of the propeller grew, filling my ears. Just like in France.

And under the growl of the engine, I heard the moans and cries of the dying. I had to get into the tunnels for safety, but I couldn't make myself step into the darkness. I pressed against the gritty sandstone and squeezed my eyes shut so I wouldn't have to see the faces of dying soldiers lurking just beyond the edge of the light: men who had needed my help; men whom I couldn't save.

"I'm sorry," I choked out.

The dankness filled my lungs. I couldn't get enough air. I whimpered, choking in dirt and blood, waiting for the bombs to fall.

"Tenny! What happened?"

I straightened and blinked at the brightness. My younger brother, Javier, stared at me in concern from the top of the dirt ramp.

"I... I looked up, and the sun hurt my eyes." I clicked off the flashlight.

He jogged past me, into the nightmare of ghosts in the cellar, and loped back up the dirt ramp, a bottle of peaches in each hand. He didn't smell the blood or hear the screams of the dying.

The buzz of the plane faded into the horizon.

"You sure you're okay, Ten?"

"Yeah." My voice caught.

I had almost done it. Were it not for that plane, I would have faced the darkness on my own. One day, I would march in there and snap my fingers at the ghosts of France. One day.

He held up the bottled peaches. "Let's go, then."

I was too glad to turn my back on my terror and follow him into the summer heat of the southern Utah desert. Outside the root cellar, all was color: red sand, thin green Lombardy poplars standing guard along the canal, blue sky stretching over the Arizona Strip to the south. The sun brought warmth back to my cheeks. In the distance, Papa's cattle hunted for browse among the sagebrush and our crops basked in the light. The heat and the wind washed everything clean. France and its ghosts were just the echoes of a nightmare.

"Did you see the plane a minute ago?" I asked Javier.

"Yeah." His eyes lit up. "I hope there's another war soon so I get a chance to fly one!"

I wrapped my arms around myself. No. I would not let war tear into my family again.

Our adobe house rose from the landscape like one of the red hills to the north. A Model T bounced away down the dirt trail that served as a road to our homestead. It looked like LeVon Banks, the mail carrier. I hurried forward, forcing Javier to keep pace with me.

We stepped through the green-painted door. The scent of roasting beef and onions wafted around us. Javier set the peaches on the table where our grandmother rolled out pie dough.

"Here you are, Abuelita." He kissed her on the cheek, using the distraction to snag a bit of the pastry.

"*Ay, qué malo!*"

She smacked at his hand, and he grinned and popped the dough into his mouth.

Abuela's gaze fell on my blue tunic dress. Red dirt from the sandstone stuck to the cloth and under my nails. I tried to brush myself off. She gave me a worried glance and returned to rolling out the crust.

"Javi, if you keep stealing the dough, there won't be enough left for the pie," Mother said without looking up.

A stack of mail sat on the counter, near where my mother stirred a pot on the oil-burning stove. I slid closer to the letters.

"Hortencia, wash up and get back to work on those potatoes."

I was only Hortencia when I was in trouble. I had graduated from Dixie College and served with the Red Cross, but on Mother's orders, I hurried to pump some water into the sink and wash my hands. One did not disobey a redhead, and especially not one who can run a homestead in the desert of southern Utah.

My brother stuck his tongue out at me as he sauntered into the living room. As I tied an apron over my dress, Papa stepped through the door. At a glance from Mother, he pulled off his dusty Stetson. He gave Abuela a kiss on the cheek, then swept my mother into an embrace.

"Carlos! The potatoes will burn." But she was smiling, her blue eyes fixed on his hazel ones.

He spun her back to the stove and picked up the mail. "I saw LeVon on his way out. He says George Chamberlain is making a fortune with his buffalo herd."

"Buffalo!" Mother shook her head, freeing a few wisps of red hair from her bun. "Always something new. We do fine with cattle."

If only saying it would make it true, but even Mother's stubbornness couldn't stop the prices from dropping or the creditors from knocking.

Father frowned. "The market is worse since the war ended." He flipped through the letters. "Ha! This is for you, *mija*."

He set a few letters aside—bills we couldn't pay—and held the thick envelope out to me.

I glanced at Mother. She grunted then called, "Javi, come in here and cut potatoes!"

"*Mamá*! Why?"

"Because you're not doing anything useful."

Javi trudged back into the kitchen. "I was helping Rosie with her radio."

"You were getting in her way," Mother said.

I smirked at my brother and handed him the apron. Abuela giggled as he scowled and tied it on. I took the mail to the living room, where María del Rosario, the middle child of our family at age seventeen, fiddled with the wires on her crystal radio. She didn't look up as I settled in a wooden chair in front of the hutch displaying jars of colored sand and striped pieces of petrified wood. I pulled open the secretary desk and spread the folded letters in front of me.

They all began, "Dear Miss Grace." That was me. Miss Grace. The editor of the *Kane County Report*, Barry Hansen, thought people were more likely to trust the advice of a Miss Grace than a Miss Hortencia Mateo, and he was probably right. Besides, this way I was as anonymous to them as they were to me. I unfolded the problems of Kane County one by one.

Dear Miss Grace, My son has taken up smoking. Is he going to ruin his health?

He'll smell like an ashtray, at least.

Dear Miss Grace, My daughter wants to bob her hair.

It's more practical than keeping it long.

Dear Miss Grace, I can't get my new radio to work.

Hmm. Maybe Rosie could help with that one.

I would put time and thought into each answer and try to make them sound witty as well. I wasn't really qualified to dispense advice. I had taken a couple of child psychology courses at Dixie College, but my degree was in home economics like most girls, with the Red Cross nursing classes thrown in for good measure. The newspaper had a note reminding readers that the advice was just for entertainment. Barry Hansen knew me at Dixie College, though, and liked my articles in the school paper, so he decided it was a good deal for both of us: I would have a job to help combat the growing stack of bills, and he would have another reason for people to buy the paper.

I unfolded the next letter and had to read it twice to be sure I understood what I saw through the poor spelling and blocky handwriting.

Dear Miss Grace, What do you do with a secrit that mite git someone killed?

CHAPTER TWO

I turned the paper over to stare at the blank back, searching for some indication that this was a joke. Not finding any answers there, I read the rest.

I found out somethin dangerus. I dont want no one else to git hurt but I dont want to git hurt neither. The police wont listin to the likes of me and if I tell someone else they could git in trouble to. What can I do?

Trouble in Boots

I sat back hard against the chair, trying not to gape. It had to be a prank. No one would write to an advice columnist on a life or death matter.

I stuffed Trouble in Boots into a cubby in the secretary desk and pulled out fresh paper to begin my responses to the real letters. Smoking. What was something helpful to say about smoking? I tapped my fountain pen on the paper and stared at the Trouble in Boots letter taunting me from its cubby hole.

If I were desperate and alone, where would I turn for help? I glanced at Rosie, hunched over the radio.

"Dinner!" Mother called.

I dropped my pen, dripping ink on the fresh paper. Rosie sighed and took off her headphones, and we gathered with the rest of the family around the linen-draped table in the kitchen. Mother's china plates displayed the roast beef and fried new potatoes from our garden.

"You see those potatoes?" Javi asked, snapping a napkin open and plopping it on his lap. "Cut perfectly."

Abuela chuckled and shook her head. Mother rolled her eyes.

"We are very proud, *mijo*," Father said with mock seriousness. "First thing Monday, we'll tell Betty Lou she can send Matilda packing and hire you for the diner."

"Ha!" Javi speared a potato and took a bite. "Even Matilda never made potatoes this good."

"Prayer first!" Mother said.

Javi grinned and set down his fork.

"Javi can say it," Papa said.

Abuela and Rosie crossed themselves in unison. Then Javi asked a quick blessing on the food, barely saying "amen" before he scooped up more potatoes and a large slice of roast beef.

"How's the radio going?" Father asked Rosie.

She launched into an erudite explanation of coils and grounds while the rest of us ate. I half listened, picking at my meat. Was there really someone asking for my help? What did he expect me to do?

"Tenny, is something wrong?" Papa asked.

I gave a start and looked up to find my family watching me. "It's one of the Miss Grace letters, but it's probably a joke."

"What does it say?" Mother asked.

I hurried to fetch the letter and passed it around.

"Definitely a joke," Rosie said. "And not a funny one."

Mother studied the paper. "I don't know. I think if he was trying to trick you, he would have given more details."

"But what kind of secret could get someone killed?" Javi asked.

Rosie and I exchanged glances. Javi had been too young to understand much about the revolution in Colonia Juárez, but we remembered the secrets. The scent of fresh dirt as we buried our money and silver in the garden and planted over it with flowers. The prickly jabs of the chokecherry bushes where we hid from the soldiers—military and revolutionary.

"Was there a return address on the envelope?" Papa asked.

"The newspaper collects the letters and sends them to me."

"Maybe they would know where it came from then."

I nodded. "I'll go to Kanab on Monday and find out."

"*Ten cuidado,*" Abuela said softly. "Secrets can be dangerous."

She looked down at her plate. Her secrets came all the way from Spain during the Carlist uprisings against the government. She never spoke of those times that had forced her from her childhood home among the orange groves of Valencia to the temporary safety of the Mexican desert.

"I'll be careful, Abuelita. I just want to make sure this man gets help."

"Why would Marshal Little not listen to him?" Javi asked.

"He might be Indian," Father said, looking again at the letter.

I nodded. We only had one marshal for the struggling town of Pahreah and environs, and he often expressed disdain for the local Paiutes and Navajo. Luckily, his job mostly involved penning stray animals and preventing gambling on horse races. Kanab had Sheriff Moore, though, and he seemed fair and competent.

"If you're going to town, can you buy some eighteen-gauge wire?" Rosie asked. "It will make a better antenna than the sixteen gauge I'm using."

"Of course," I said. I would stop by the general store and Barry Hansen's place in Kanab and then see if any Paiutes or Navajo were in town and willing to talk to me.

After dessert and dishes, everyone gathered in the living room to enjoy the last of the evening light casting a rosy glow through the window. Even our sheepdog Daisy sprawled out next to the coffee table, belly up and begging for a scratch.

I obliged her then picked up my pen and pulled a fresh sheet of paper from the desk. Mother darned socks and Rosie put on her earphones to search for transmissions on the crystal radio, stopping to listen when she found faint Morse code messages. While she adjusted the antenna wire, Papa sat at the salterio and put the metal picks on his fingers to pluck the strings. Javi tuned his guitar, and they played together, filling the room with upbeat songs of love and Western deserts and valleys. Mother occasionally added her sweet Gaelic voice to the harmony.

When Papa took a break, Javier moved away from the traditional Spanish and Mexican songs to fingerpick "Royal Garden Blues." Mother tapped her foot to the jazz tune, but Papa frowned. And when Javi played "How Ya Gonna Keep 'Em Down on the Farm After They've Seen Paree," Mother scowled, too.

"Music!" Rosie gestured us over. "I'm picking up music!"

Javi cut off his playing, and we all crowded around the radio, taking turns with the earphones. Someone was broadcasting their own Dixieland tune played on a trumpet and clarinet.

"Rosie, you have to rig it so I can do that!" Javi said. "How far away do you suppose they are? California?"

"I bet it's coming from Dixie College," Rosie said with a longing glance at her simple crystal radio. "I'd need vacuum tubes and a battery to transmit."

Javi grabbed his guitar. "Well, if they're that close, I'll go join their band, and we'll get famous together."

He launched into "Fidgety Feet."

Abuela clapped as he navigated the tricky chords, but Mother and I exchanged a worried look. The world out there was a dangerous place. Politicians and captains of industry throwing men's lives away in wars, factories, and mines. Revolutionaries and anarchists sowing chaos and fear of immigrants. Only here, among the red and vermillion cliffs, were we safe.

The Trouble in Boots letter accused me from the desk, but I shoved it farther into its cubby and shut my eyes, glad when Papa began again on the salterio.

CHAPTER THREE

I woke the next morning to a flood of scents from bacon, biscuits, and tortilla española cooking. I groaned. It was Sunday. Mother and Abuela were at it again.

I pulled a poplin skirt and chiffon blouse with a wide collar over my corset and snuck out to peek in the kitchen.

An iron silence divided the two women, broken only by the sizzle from the frying pans. Abuela smacked a plate of sliced cured jamón down in the center of the table. Mother narrowed her eyes and scooted the jamón over to give the bacon the place of honor. Abuela pushed the bacon aside for the tortilla española. Mother triumphantly nudged those out of the way and crowned the table with biscuits and gravy.

Papa came up beside me, and we shared a grim look.

"It all smells delicious," he said a little too cheerfully.

Rosie and Javier joined us, and we gathered around the table for Papa to say the prayer. Then each of us carefully took equal amounts of Mother and Abuela's offerings.

"This bacon is just right," Papa said, quickly adding, *"y el jamón es muy sabroso, Mamá!"*

I scooped the fried potatoes and eggs of the tortilla española onto Mother's biscuits and ate a forkful. "Mmmm!"

Javier, with the hearty appetite of a fourteen-year-old boy, finished first.

"*Come! Come!*" Abuela said, offering him the tortilla. "You're too skinny."

"Have some more biscuits, Javi," Mother said at the same time.

"I'll have more of everything," Javi said quickly.

"And for later, *hay magdalenas*," Abuela said.

"And pudding," Mother added.

I tried not to groan. I had to be careful to leave exactly the same amount of biscuits and tortilla on my plate so I didn't have to take seconds of either. At least we wouldn't get hungry during church.

Church. Almost everyone in Pahreah would be there, and one of them might have a deadly secret if I believed Trouble in Boots.

"We need to get ready for sacrament meeting." Mother looked around the table, a challenge in her eyes.

Abuela pinched her lips together and glared at the platter of biscuits. Rosie pushed her tortilla around with her fork.

Papa rose. "I'll get my tie on."

"Javi," Abuela said quickly. "You should stay. We will pray to San Vicente *y* La Virgen de Guadalupe. Perhaps Casimiro will visit, eh? You like his stories. *Muy entretenidos.*"

Javi smiled. "But Abuelita, all the girls at church would miss me."

"*Eres hijo de tu padre!*" Abuela said. "*Mormonitas!* We can go to Mass in Monticello soon. You'll meet nice girls. *Católicas.*"

"But *we* are not Catholic," Mother said, standing quickly.

I stared down at the china plate. Mother's grandmother had carried the china across the plains to Utah, and my grandmother—my *other* grandmother—had brought it with her to Colonia Juárez. The china was the only thing Mother had managed to bring when we fled the revolution. An important link to my past. Half of my past.

"I'll help you clean up," I offered.

"No," Rosie said quietly. "I'll do it so you can get ready."

Mother frowned but nodded at this olive branch. When she was younger, Rosie loved going to Pahreah, bragging about how it rhymed with the first part of her name, María. Now, she would go on the long rides with Abuela to attend Mass in Monticello a few times a year, but she dug in her heels at the short trip to town for LDS meetings. I attended both. They both felt comfortable, like two different sets of shoes I had grown accustomed to.

In the faint tension still hovering over the dinner table, Mother and I got our hats and gloves. We waited outside while Papa and Javi fetched the Model T, giving me a moment to breathe in the sweet fragrance of the roses Papa and I toiled over each summer.

The Model T made the drive northeast from the homestead fly by in a cloud of dust. It was much more convenient than when we had to hook up the wagon, but the Model T seemed like an extravagant luxury now that the wartime boom was over. We passed several abandoned farmhouses along the way, their canals gone dry, and the fences grey and splintered by the southern Utah sun. Once prices for beef fell, it was like a domino tipped over, bumping the next and the next and pushing many of our neighbors to Kanab, Salt Lake City, or even the golden promise of California.

We turned northward to Pahreah proper, and the car bounded over the rough road. Red hills blocked the view, then fell away to reveal the sharp drop into the river valley below. I gripped the edge of the car as we wound our way down the steep lane, the tires rumbling near the edge.

The little town of adobe buildings sat at the base of steep slopes striped with sandstone of orange, dusky purple, white, and pale green, like a village guarded by colorful pyramids.

We parked and walked into the adobe brick building that served as a schoolhouse and meeting hall for the dwindling families of Pahreah. It was the same each week, though the congregation slowly shrank. This week, though, I was looking for secrets.

Marshal Little strutted around the room, whispering with his cronies. Papa stopped to talk with some other farmers and stockmen. Mother nodded greetings to Sister Briggs, who had grown up in the colonies with her polygamist father dodging the federal marshals, and exchanged a few words with the Chamberlain family, who had been our neighbors in Mexico until the Revolution sent us all fleeing for safety in El Paso. They had a daughter, Sytha, just a couple of years younger than me, but I never had much to say to her. It was still strange seeing them in Utah.

Bo Young, who owned the homestead next to ours, sauntered over to elbow Papa. His skin was wrinkled and red from long days in the sun, like a wild turkey's wattle. "I hear some families are packing up to try their luck in Colonia Juárez again," he boomed. "Are you planning on going down home and letting me take over your place?"

Papa shook his head firmly, and Mother glared at Bo. "This *is* our home."

Bo grinned like a coyote. "You might as well sell now, while you can still get a good price."

Papa took Mother's arm and led her away before her temper exploded.

Bo Young was someone I easily imagined hiding a whole herd of secrets.

Bo's son Mel stood near his father. He flushed at his father's rudeness, which set off the pale flesh color of his tin mask shaped into a nose and held in place by false spectacles. I hadn't seen him without the tin mask, but I had witnessed enough other men missing noses, ears, or parts of their jaw from the Great War to guess at the scars his facial prosthetic disguised. At least I had some idea of what Mel wanted to hide.

"Tenny!"

Ginny Hamblin breezed over to me. She had kisses for my cheeks and a nasty look for Bo Young. Tall and boyishly thin, sporting a blonde bob and a swishing, low-waisted dress, she had been born for the current fashions. The same styles made me feel like a lumpy pillow stuffed into a flour sack. Yet, during the week, she donned overalls to work alongside the men she hired on her homestead.

"How is your garden?" she asked.

"Wonderful. The Honorine de Brabant rose is blooming this year, and it has amazing dark pink stripes."

"How delicious!" Ginny's brown eyes sparkled. "I already have some nice pumpkins. They're going to be big ones. We'll be ready for the fair this year, won't we?"

I grinned and nodded. I was happy to grow the roses for myself—and for the time I got to share with Papa—but Ginny's competitiveness was contagious.

Sam Ellis lingered behind Ginny, half listening. When thinking of the Indians in town, I had almost forgotten Sam. He had been raised by a Mormon family in Fredonia on the Arizona Strip after his Paiute parents died, and now he worked for Ginny on her homestead. Since he attended church, most of the town accepted him as a "Lamanite brother." But if he knew something dangerous, would they take him seriously? His handwriting was better than Trouble in Boots', but he was friendly with some of the Paiutes and Navajo in the area.

"Morning, Sister Mateo." Sam said when he caught me watching him.

I shook his hand. "Have you been well, Brother Ellis?"

"Well as can be."

"No 'troubles'?" I prodded, looking for a sign of guilty recognition.

He and Ginny both gave me a curious look.

"Short on water like everyone else," he said warily. "You all right, Sister Mateo?"

"Oh, yes, fine." Just a clumsy detective. "They're getting ready for the opening prayer. We'd better sit."

I joined my family on our customary bench toward the back. Ginny and Sam sat as well, sharing a bench but far enough apart to avoid the town's gossip. Ginny was a single woman who—if rumor was true—had turned down several marriage proposals, and Sam wasn't much older than her and a very loyal employee.

The congregation sang "Tradition and Error in Battle Array," and I flinched at the words, "They're onward to conquer or die on the field." Most of the congregation sang on, not forced to remember the sounds and stench of death in the trenches. I relaxed when the young men prayed over the bread and water and passed the sacrament around.

I should have been thinking holy thoughts, but my mind kept

coming back to more immediate concerns, like if one of my neighbors was hiding something dangerous behind their Sunday best and bowed head.

The water came in little glass cups, and I gladly sipped from one. Not long ago, we'd all drunk from the same large chalice, leaving those at the back to sample the flavors of other people's licorice and spearmint gum, trying to avoid the odd mustache hair floating in the water. The individual cups were the only good thing to come of the influenza epidemic of the past two winters. February had been a grim month in Kane County.

The speaker who took the pulpit after the sacrament was remembering the epidemic, too. Plague. Revolutions and war. Anarchists among us. He predicted that the Second Coming of Christ was imminent and exhorted us to be prepared.

"And even now, the Lamanites are coming to a knowledge of the truth!" He gestured to Sam and then to Papa with his mestizo heritage. "Soon, they will become a fair and delightsome people as prophesied."

Mother clenched her fists, her cheeks flushed with spots of anger. She shifted as if to stand, but Papa put a hand on her arm.

I sank down in the pew. Our family was not a Sunday School lesson. I loved Papa's skin—deep brown from long hours working in the sun—though I hated the suspicious way strangers often looked at him. I appreciated that my skin didn't sunburn as quickly as other girls', too. Yet I was grateful to blend into southern Utah's Anglo population better than Papa did, even if I sometimes felt like a traitor because of it.

As soon as the meeting was over, Papa guided Mother out of the church.

Javi chuckled and whispered, "You look pale, Ten. I guess you're becoming more 'fair and delightsome' already."

"Hmph!" I smiled a little, wishing I could find the humor in the situation as easily as he did.

As we exited the chapel on our parents' heels, Javi said, "Did you hear? There's a prospector up looking for gold in the canyons again. I want to go, too."

I rolled my eyes. "There's real work to do on the homestead."

"But imagine what we could do with all that gold!"

"They've only found a little gold dust out there, and that's something to be grateful for. Turning Pahreah into a boom-and-bust town isn't a real solution."

Javi frowned and shoved his hands deep in his pockets.

Just let him forget it. Gold was a dangerous thing. I hesitated and remembered the letter. Possibly dangerous enough to get someone killed.

As we climbed into the Model T, I glanced back and saw Ginny and Sam walking toward her car, engaged in friendly conversation and apparently unaware of the raised eyebrows and questioning glances following them. A man could hire all the ranch hands he needed, Paiute or not, Mormon or not, but in Ginny's case, well, whispers flew behind false smiles. And Sam was her most respectable ranch hand. At least, he showed up at church on Sundays. Some of the others were drifters, just looking for work as they passed through. I didn't want to give the gossips any credit, but maybe it was risky for Ginny. It certainly wasn't a secret, though.

Mother caught my worried look and squeezed my arm. "You're concerned about your friend?"

"Do you think it's safe for her to live alone like that?"

"Virginia Hamblin can take care of herself."

I nodded, hoping she was right.

CHAPTER FOUR

Monday morning, I woke up as Papa went out to milk the cows. Kanab waited for me with its potential answers about Trouble in Boots. But Monday was washing day. Nothing short of an act of God could put off the inevitability of laundry. I dressed and hurried into the kitchen where Mother already had water boiling on the stove. I glanced out the window at the rising sun and shot an imploring look at Mother.

She sighed. "You get it started, and then you can run into town while we finish up."

"Thank you!"

I hauled the buckets of hot water outside. The steam billowed around me in the cool of the morning and made my cotton dress stick to my skin. I poured the water into the hand-powered washing machine along with soap flakes and light-colored clothes carrying a fine layer of red dust. I turned the agitator wheel so fast that my hand cramped up and I had to shake it out.

This beat scrubbing the clothes on a washboard, but someday, we would have an electric washing machine. Someday, Kane County would have electricity.

Rosie and Mother came out with buckets of rinse water. I gave them quick kisses on the cheek and hurried inside to change my soaked dress. On my way back out, I ran into Papa putting the milk in the icebox.

"Off so early?" he asked.

"I want to go before it gets too hot."

"You're worried about that letter?"

I nodded. "The man who wrote it... Even if I find him, what am I going to do? I try to help, but..." I swallowed hard, fighting the impulse to squeeze my eyes shut because if I did, I would see France again and all the men I had not been able to help.

"Oh, *mija*, it hurts to feel powerless. I saw it in the revolution and then in the mines. It's why I couldn't work there."

I smiled thinly. "I thought you just hated the cold."

When we first came to Utah from Colonia Juárez, Papa found work in Jesse Knight's mines in Silver City, but Mother didn't want to raise us in a mining town, even one run by a Mormon. Papa liked to say they chased the warm weather south until the Grand Canyon stood in their way, so they turned around to claim their homestead back across the Utah border near Pahreah. But there was another problem with moving any farther south: Arizona. Mother and Papa's marriage might be called into question in a state where whites could only marry other whites. And we children—we would not legally be allowed to marry anyone, being neither Mexican nor white.

"I do hate the snow." Papa chuckled. "But I also hated being dependent on other people. Sometimes I wonder, though, if I should have stayed, organized with the unions, spoken up for better working conditions across Utah."

"Would it have made a difference?"

"I don't know. But we shouldn't be so afraid of failing that we don't try."

I saw again the faces of dead men—boys—who had cried for their mothers as gas rolled around them or their blood seeped out of limbs shattered by artillery.

I shook my head. "Trying isn't enough."

I kissed him on the cheek and grabbed my bonnet. I would sometimes ride my bike to town—walking it through the sand drifts—but this morning I opted for speed and cranked up the Model T. I motored past Bo Young's place where the canal carried water to his crops and cattle like an artery. To the north, farther uphill, Ginny Hamblin's place looked too still, like the abandoned homesteads. Her branch of the creek had run dry, and brown crept over her fields. Bo Young probably cackled with joy every time he saw it.

The only movement in the landscape was a pair of stray brown-and-white Hereford steers on the road, and they bore Bo's circle "Y" brand. I stopped to let them meander back across from Ginny's, where a downed fence rail had given them access. Probably, they had found that the grazing was better at home.

Sweat trickled under my collar by the time I approached Kanab, the little wood and adobe buildings clustered below the red cliffs. I rode past Mrs. Halliday's ice cream shop and Betty Lou's, where the enticing scents of pancakes and bacon drifted from the open door. Ha. Javi was a long way from replacing Betty Lou's cook.

I parked the Model T and climbed out. Casimiro Fernandez, one of the Spanish shepherds who worked for local families, strolled out of Betty Lou's, patting his stomach. He usually stayed out on the range with the sheep, but when he was around Pahreah, he always stopped by our homestead for Abuela's cooking.

"*Hola!*" he called to me. "*Que tal?*"

"*Bien.* I'm surprised to see you in town."

"Mr. Chamberlain sent me on a few errands. Give your abuela *besos* from me."

"I will. *Adios!*"

"*Luego.*"

The Spanish coloring our conversation earned us a suspicious look from a lady leaving Betty Lou's. I wanted to pretend not to notice or to care, but I hunched my shoulders a little as I hurried down the road.

"Miss Mateo!" the mail carrier, LeVon Banks, called from his truck.

He parked and hopped out, waving at me with a handful of letters and telegrams ready for delivery. White stubble scruffed his chin, but he was wiry and spry. I paused, and he scurried to catch up. A gold tooth glinted in his mouth when he smiled.

"Has your father considered adding some buffalo on your property? I know a fellow trying to sell some. Your folks will get a great bargain, my friend will unload some buffalo he can't feed, and I'll just take a small cut. Winners all around." He grinned.

I smiled back. "Sorry, Mr. Banks. My father is old-fashioned. He's not sure about buffalo."

"Oh, well. Someone will take me up on the deal." He nodded back at Betty Lou's place. "Now, I wish I could get her to listen to me. This country has got all these people who can afford cars now, driving out to see sites like the Grand Canyon and this new national park at Zion. We've gotta get them to stop in Kane County. Spread some of their money around. Here's my idea: Betty Lou makes delicious fried onions. Best I've ever had. So, what if she redesigned her restaurant to look like a giant onion?"

"A giant *onion*?" I glanced back at the innocent-looking restaurant, trying to imagine LeVon's vision, and shuddered in silent horror.

"Sure, like them Russian palaces you see pictures of in the news. Then, on the way to the Grand Canyon, people could stop to eat at the Grand Kane-Onion!"

LeVon hooted at his own joke, and I forced a chuckle. "It might flow off the tongue better abbreviated as the Grand Kane 'Yon"

"Thanks! I knew you were a smart girl. Good with words. Barry Hansen's got you doing something over there at the paper, doesn't he?"

The polite smile froze on my face. LeVon handled all the letters going back and forth in Kane County. He could easily guess I was Miss Grace, and then everyone would know. That would end my employment and embarrass my family as people turned awkward toward us. "I just do some proofreading for him."

"Proofing! That makes sense. You're clever. Went to college and everything. One of these days, maybe he'll make you a real reporter."

Still chuckling to himself, he strolled on. I walked in the other direction, a little sorry I was going to miss Betty Lou's expression when she heard about the Grand Kane 'Yon.

Barry Hansen ran the *Kane County Report* from the back of his red brick house. I skirted the long Victorian porch with its climbing roses—he would be among my competition at the fair, but none of his blooms were as big as mine this year—and knocked on the back door.

Barry's wife Myrtle poked her head out, brown hair frizzing free of her braid. The scent of ink rolled out around her. "Sister Mateo!" She lowered her voice. "You have the letters already?"

"I actually had a question about one of them."

"This isn't a good time," Myrtle said, glancing over her shoulder. "Barry's busy with a big story. A tragedy."

My chest tightened. "What happened?"

Myrtle leaned closer. "Someone's been murdered."

"Who?" The word came out scratchy and dry.

"I don't remember his name. One of Virginia Hamblin's ranch hands."

The ground tilted beneath me, and I braced myself against the doorframe. Somewhere, almost on the edge of hearing, dying men screamed for help in the dark. I was too late. Too late again. Someone had reached out to be saved, and I failed him.

"Was it Sam Ellis?" I whispered.

Myrtle shook her head.

"Is Ginny all right?"

Myrtle squeezed her hands together. "I... I don't think so. They're asking if she might be the one who did it."

"Ginny! If she did, it must have been self-defense."

"He was shot in the back of the head. In the bunkhouse. I know some people question her... well, being a single woman, and keeping those men around, but it doesn't seem like her."

"Not at all. What about the other ranch hands?"

"They were out chasing down some stray cattle. They don't know why this fellow wasn't with them."

"What does Ginny say?"

"Says she heard the shot and found him dead, but it doesn't look good. Sheriff Moore's out there now."

If the dead man was Trouble in Boots, the letter didn't matter anymore. At the moment, my friend needed my help.

"I should go," I said.

I hurried back to the Model T. There were no dangerous secrets at Ginny's homestead, were there? No, it was too far-fetched.

I drove back to the Hamblin place and turned up the lane leading to the house. A crowd from town had already gathered: Sheriff Moore, his deputies, Marshal Little, Barry Hansen, and several curious onlookers. The only ones who took any notice of my approach were a few steers with Ginny's rocking boot brand on their sides.

I braked and stared at the brand. Trouble in Boots. Was the man trying to tell me who he was? Or who he was in danger from?

When I parked and climbed out, I found Mother among the small crowd, a basket hanging from her elbow. I didn't have to ask why she was there. Mother was doing what Mormon women did when someone was in trouble: bringing food. I wiggled past the other curious neighbors to stand beside her.

Barry Hansen was jotting notes on a little pad of paper. Bo Young's ruddy face crinkled in glee as he surveyed the property. He was probably hoping Ginny would have to go to jail so she wouldn't be able to prove up her homestead and he could snatch it up.

Ginny stood on her porch with her arms crossed, her blonde bob tidy, her overalls as clean as if she were modeling them for the Sears catalog. She faced off with the sheriff, almost tall enough to meet him eye to eye.

"If I shot him, I would tell you I shot him! You think because I'm a lady I can't handle a gun?"

"No, Sister Hamblin, I know you can..."

"You think I'm too addled to realize when I pulled the trigger?"

"No, Sister—"

"Then you either think I'm a liar or that I get all hysterical when I have to shoot at somebody. You remember that cougar I took down?"

"Well, yes."

"I've never been more scared in my life than when I shot that critter, and I didn't have amnesia over that, now, did I?"

"I suppose not, but—"

"But what?"

"We don't have any other suspects."

Ginny gave an indelicate snort. "Then find one. That's your job, not mine. But I'm not going anywhere with you unless you've got a warrant, and you ain't gonna get one, because I didn't do anything wrong."

Sheriff Moore frowned. "I still have to ask you not to leave the area—"

Ginny threw her hands up. "Oh, fine. I wasn't planning on going anywhere anyhow. Now get off my porch. You leave too, Bo Young, you good-for-nothing cuss."

Bo smirked and stomped off, and the sheriff returned to his inspection of the neighboring wooden bunkhouse with his deputies and Marshal Little.

"Sister Mateo!" Ginny motioned Mother over and accepted the basket of biscuits and jar of gravy. "You're too kind."

Ginny sounded sincere, and for all her bravado, her hands trembled as she gripped the handle of the woven basket.

"Not at all," Mother said and lowered her voice. "Do you want to tell me about it?"

"There's not much to tell. I heard a bang this morning. I figured someone had shot a coyote or some of the jackrabbits pestering the crops. I found Roy in the bunkhouse. There was. . ." she swallowed hard. "There was a lot of blood, but he was still warm. I fetched Dr. Norris from Kanab. I never imagined they'd suspect me." She sat heavily on the porch steps and stared at the bunkhouse before turning her face to the hills on the far side of her property.

I sat next to her. "Who was he? I don't think I knew any Roy."

"He hadn't been around that long. He drifted into town, looking for work. He was handy—worked hard, good at fixing things. He'd worked at a factory or something up north."

"Why did he come way out here?" I asked quietly.

"I didn't ask. Not my business. My only concern was that he got the work done and didn't try to cheat me."

I would have thought it was none of my business, too. Except that he might have been the one who asked for my help. There was nothing I could do for him now. Another ghost to haunt me.

Mother said a few more consoling words to Ginny and offered to help her clean up the bunkhouse.

"They said to leave it be since they're still investigating." Her voice hitched. "Unless someone comes for the body, though, the sheriff will need help laying it out. They won't let me close to it."

I glanced back at the bunkhouse. Ginny wasn't a killer. That meant someone else in Kane County was. And if Roy had died for his secret, I was the only one who knew anything about it.

CHAPTER FIVE

As soon as Mother and I arrived home, I dashed inside and pulled the Trouble in Boots letter from its cubby. I couldn't keep this to myself. I also couldn't waste gasoline driving back and forth to Kanab every day, so I scrambled to finish my Dear Miss Grace letters.

Rosie had been using my paper to transcribe Morse code messages. *I'm in Panguitch how far can you hear me?* Too bad we couldn't respond. *Meet me tonight usual place.* Some scandal brewing there! *And it came to pass that I did go forth and partake of the fruit...* Good heavens! Someone was broadcasting the *Book of Mormon* in Morse code. I wasn't sure if that was admirable devotion or insanity.

I finished off the Miss Grace letters and ran outside past the laundry flapping on the line.

"I'll be back again soon," I called to Abuela, who was picking peas in the garden. "*Besos!*" I blew her a kiss.

She waved, and I cranked up the Model T and drove off. Even with the top up, the black seats absorbed the desert heat, filling the car with the scent of warm leather and a heat that made the blowing dust stick to me.

When I passed Ginny's place, the homestead looked quiet, but low hills shielded the bunkhouse from the road. Hopefully, Sheriff Moore would be back in town. I didn't want everyone to know I was Miss Grace if I could help it.

I stopped by Barry's place first, and this time he answered the door. Ink smudged his fingers.

"I have those letters," I told him.

"Good, come in, come in." He straightened his loose tie and gestured around the print shop. Trays of moveable type sat on every flat surface. "I'm afraid everything else is taking a backseat to this murder case."

"Has the sheriff made any progress?"

"Maybe. There was a prospector in town a few days ago. Wanted to try his hand at that gold vein from a few years back. Sheriff's organized a search for the man to see if he had anything to do with Roy."

"Is there any reason to suspect they knew each other?"

Barry shrugged. "They're both outsiders."

It was a flimsy connection, but it must have been an outsider who killed Roy. How could one of our neighbors have done such a thing? At least the sheriff wasn't looking at Ginny anymore.

I pulled the note from my purse. "I got this with the other letters. I wonder if it has anything to do with the... the murder. It talks about a secret. Maybe Roy found out about the gold vein, and the prospector wanted to keep it a secret."

Barry read over the letter and nodded. "Could be."

"Do you still have the envelope the letter came in?"

Barry rubbed the scruff on his face and glanced ruefully around the shop. "I doubt it. You ought to show Sheriff Moore, though. It might shed some new light on the case."

"You're right."

I hurried across the street to the sheriff's office. I knocked on his office door and found him at his desk, writing out a telegram and looking harried.

"Sister Mateo," he said crisply. "What can I do for you?"

"Barry Hansen wanted you to see this." I handed him the letter, keeping my Miss Grace identity out of the conversation. "He received it at the newspaper and thought it might have something to do with the case. He was too busy to come himself."

"Huh." The sheriff peered at it through his reading spectacles. He put the letter into a drawer. "Tell Barry thank you for this additional information. When I have anything solid, I'll pass it on to him for the paper."

I clutched my purse with both hands and nodded. Why had I assumed I would get to keep the letter? Of course, the sheriff would want it. It was all out of my control now.

I walked out into the glare of the desert sun and let the door smack shut behind me. Why was I disappointed? I did not need to be responsible for anyone else's life. I walked back to the Model T.

A familiar buzz hummed over the town. Kids looked up from their games of marbles and hopscotch in the dirt, and housewives drying their hands on aprons stepped outside to glance up at the sky.

"Hide!" I wanted to scream at them. "Take cover!" But my tongue stuck to the roof of my mouth, and my feet wouldn't move.

I dropped behind the car and watched the Jenny biplane soar over, the bold 976 bright on its side and its rudder flashing its red, white, and blue. It was one of ours, but bombs didn't distinguish between friend or foe.

Something white burst out of the plane. I threw myself flat on the ground and covered my head.

No explosions. No screams. Only squeals of laughter.

I slowly straightened and looked around. Papers fluttered down to litter the street. I snatched one up and read it.

SPECTACULAR AIR SHOW
DAREDEVIL STUNTS
PREPARE TO BE AWED AND AMAZED BY THE
COURAGE AND **SKILL** OF THE AVIATOR

The kids shouted in excitement, but I crumpled the paper. Life was dangerous enough without daredevil tricks.

I drove back to the homestead, the sun pounding down on the car. In the distance, the engine of the plane made a mockery of the desert peace. The rumble seemed to be getting closer, following me. I put on the brakes and closed my eyes.

I wasn't imagining it. The sound of the plane chased me, rising in pitch. I was out in the open. No place to hide. I ducked behind the steering wheel, and the plane whirred past. The pulse hammered in my ears slowly returned to normal, and I tightened my grip on the steering wheel. Ridiculous pilot.

And he was heading for our homestead.

I pushed the car to its top speed, bouncing over the ruts and zigging around deep sand, trying—impossibly—to outrace the plane as it dipped lower. It touched down in one of our alfalfa pastures. I parked and ran to join my family, who watched in amazement as the wood-and-fabric machine bounced along the field and stuttered to a halt.

"*Madre mia!*" Abuela crossed herself.

The rest of us raced forward as the pilot climbed from the plane, but I reached him first.

"What kind of stunt is this?" I demanded.

"That wasn't a stunt, Doll," he said, grinning. His face was handsome and deeply tanned, though his flight goggles left impressions around his eyes. Blond hair stuck out from under his leather cap. "If you come to my show, you'll see real stunts. Here." He pulled out a ticket. "This one's on me, for letting me use your field."

"Letting you—"

"Whoa!" Javi walked all around the plane, his eyes wide. "This is the real monkey's mustache! What does it feel like to fly?"

I narrowed my eyes. Oh no, this trickster wasn't getting his claws into my little brother. Javi would stay on the ground where he belonged. Safe.

"What made you think we want an airplane show in Kane County?" I interrupted.

My parents gave me a confused look, and Javi scowled at me.

"I just go where the winds take me. Why, only two days ago, I was flying over the golden hills of Hollywood. Now, let me tell you—"

He walked off with my parents and brother, and I glared after him. He wasn't in Hollywood two days ago. He was flying over our homestead. So, he was a liar. And an outsider. Perhaps a murderer?

CHAPTER SIX

Victor Holbrook. That was the pilot's name. Or so he claimed. And of course, Mother invited him to dinner. At least that gave me the opportunity to dig for his real story.

As we gathered around the meal of fabada made with beans and sausage, Victor flashed his smile and jabbered about his flying feats in the war. Abuela and I were the only two who didn't neglect our bowls to soak in his every detail about barrel rolls and loop-the-loops, and Abuela just didn't trust anyone new.

"Did you ever fight the Red Baron?" Javi stared at Victor as though Babe Ruth had come to dinner, his cornbread and fabada untouched before him.

I watched Victor carefully. The Red Baron had died over Australian lines just after the first of our Air Service pilots joined the fight, but every braggart pilot had a story of near misses with the legendary flying ace.

He shrugged. "Nah, he'd been shot down before they sent me out. Greatest pilot of the war. For either side."

The man wasn't a complete liar. I had to credit him for that.

"But I was at the St. Mihiel offensive. Over a thousand planes in the sky, just for our side! It gives me chills remembering it." He drizzled honey on his cornbread. "And there was this one time. I was almost out of fuel, and there were three German Fokkers on my tail."

Victor took a bite of the cornbread. The rest of my family leaned forward in hushed anticipation. Victor swallowed the cornbread with obvious relish and grabbed Javi's fork along with his own. He glanced around and snatched the fork from my hand.

"Thanks, Doll!" He laid the forks out in formation chasing his spoon. "I didn't know if I was over their lines or ours, but I dipped down, and... bang-bang-bang!"

Mother jumped and laughed nervously.

Victor flashed a smile that probably had girls fainting over him. "I thought I'd been hit. But it was my own guys firing. One of the Fokkers rolled to the side, knocking the second plane off course." He demonstrated with the forks. "Now, it was just me and the last Boche pilot."

Javi's eyes lit with excitement as Victor maneuvered the fork so it was chasing his spoon.

"I banked right, trying to lure him over to the British anti-aircraft guns, but he got above me. There was only one thing I could do." He took the spoon and fork airborne to demonstrate. "I looped over the Fokker and came down on top of him. Pushed him right down to the ground." He dropped the fork on the table with a clank and parked his spoon safely.

"Did the plane explode?" Javi asked.

Victor's expression tightened, and he looked down at the fork. "No. In fact, the pilot survived the crash, and the Brits took him prisoner. I sent him my cigarette ration, and he sent me back his chocolate. Decent fellow."

Javi looked confused, but I studied Victor. His smile had lost some sincerity, not reaching his troubled eyes. Yes, he had his own ghosts from the war. Those pilots respected each other, and few of us really wanted to see more death by the end. About some things, at least, he was telling the truth.

Victor turned his attention to his food and mopped the last of the bean and sausage stew up with his cornbread. "This is good. What do you call it?"

"Fabada," Mother said. "Have some more."

"I won't say no to that, ma'am."

That roused Rosie and Javi, and they demonstrated appetites to rival Victors'.

When we finished eating, Javi said, "Do you want to see our crystal radio?"

"Sure," Victor said, missing the possessive look that crossed Rosie's face.

She started scooping dishes off the table as fast as possible, but I put a hand on her arm. "You go. I'll get these washed."

"Thank you!" She smiled sheepishly and hurried after Javi and Victor to keep an eye on her radio.

Papa lingered in the kitchen with me as I poured hot water from the stove into the basin to wash the dishes.

"You don't like our guest," he said, his voice low.

"I don't."

"Why not?"

"I don't think he's very honest."

"Young men do like to brag." Papa watched me as I scrub at the plates. "You don't like being reminded of the war."

I pinched my lips together and sank a cup in the warm, soapy water. "I don't." I dunked the cup in the rinse water and glanced at Papa. "Why do you ask?"

"He spoke to me before dinner. Wanted to make a business arrangement."

"He's a stranger. We don't really know—"

Papa held up a hand. "It's not risky. In fact, it's an excellent opportunity for us. He'll keep his plane here and offer rides to people in the days leading up to his airshow. We get a percentage of the profits."

"Oh." That was a good arrangement.

"But I don't want to agree if it makes you too… uncomfortable."

I rinsed a couple more cups without answering. I was never sure how much my family noticed or understood about the moments of panic that sometimes gripped me. About the nightmares that woke me trembling in the darkness. The war was supposed to be behind us. I wasn't sure it ever would be for me, but I tried to keep it to myself. I couldn't let it hurt an opportunity for my family to make extra money. Not when we needed it so much.

I wiped my hands on my apron and turned to Papa. "I don't trust Mr. Holbrook, but I don't see anything wrong with his idea as long as he pays us at the end of each day. You should do it."

"You're sure?"

I nodded.

Papa kissed me on the forehead and went into the parlor. I frowned at the sudsy water. I should be grateful that Victor had touched down in our field and not Bo Young's. Bo would squeeze every penny from this deal. It was better than one of LeVon Banks's schemes with some new breed of cattle or a crazy idea for luring tourists to stop in Kanab.

But at least those far-fetched ideas would let us rely on our own hard work instead of a fly-by-night outsider whom we couldn't trust.

I finished up the dishes and joined my family.

Rosie was searching for signals and passing the earphones to Victor when she found something. They laughed over one of the messages. Javi alternated between playing his guitar and asking for the earphones so he could listen, too.

I sat next to Mother on the sofa and picked up my knitting, trying to ignore my younger siblings scrambling for Victor's attention. He wandered the room while Rosie adjusted the antenna, pausing in front of the curio with its collection of petrified wood. My fingers tightened on the steel knitting needles.

"These are interesting," Victor said. "What are they?"

"Petrified wood." Javi stopped playing to join him. "It's all over the place here. Tenny collects it."

"Does she?" Victor grinned at me. I pretended to ignore him.

"Oh! Here's something about the murder," Rosie said.

We all paused to watch as she listened to the Morse code. Her face fell. "Nothing new. Just someone sharing the news."

"A murder?" Victor scanned our faces as if searching for a hidden joke. "Here in Kane County?"

"A ranch hand named Roy Shelton," Javi said.

Victor shifted as if the name gave him a little electric shock. "What? A dispute over a girl or something?"

"Nobody knows yet," Javi said. "It just happened this morning."

Victor frowned. "That's a shame."

He knew something. Roy's name, at least, though perhaps not that the man was dead. And the sheriff was looking for an outsider.

"Why did you say you decided to come to Kane County, Mr. Holbrook?" I asked, my knitting needles clicking on.

He shrugged. "You folks ever see an air show here before?"

"Never," Javi said.

"That's a good enough reason for me."

I kept my eyes on my knitting. Kane County was out of the way. A good place to lie low if someone wanted to avoid trouble. But we didn't need them bringing trouble with them.

A rapid knock sounded on the front door.

Mother quickly set her knitting aside to answer it. Josh Brown, the son of the local women's Relief Society president, stood at the door.

"Sister Mateo!" he said, trying to catch his breath. "Ma needs your help."

Mother grabbed her hat. "What's wrong?"

"They found the prospector everyone was looking for. He's dead, and Ma's laying out the body as soon as the sheriff gets done with him."

CHAPTER SEVEN

My gaze shot to Victor, but this time he gave no sign of recognition or guilt. Just vague interest.

I set down my knitting. "I'm coming too."

Mother made no objection. I had seen enough dead bodies on the Western Front that there was nothing left to shelter me from, and it was an act of charity to prepare a stranger's body for burial. Plus, Sheriff Moore might have something to say that would ease my conscience over Roy.

We drove over the bumpy road to Sister Brown's house, Josh sitting solemnly in the back seat. He led us to the door of the barn, but Sister Brown shooed him away. "This is no sight for a young boy."

Josh pouted and kicked a rock away from the barn, but he wandered back to the house under Sister Brown's stern eye.

Dr. Norris exited the barn, his face grim.

Sister Brown gave us a weak smile. "Thank you for coming so quickly. This might be a bit much for some of the sisters, but you've seen enough in your days…"

That said something about the condition of the body. The women of Kane County were no shrinking violets. Mother and I exchanging a bracing look.

"What happened to him?" Mother asked.

Sister Brown just handed us handkerchiefs to tie over our noses and gestured us inside. We stepped into the barn, which was bright with kerosene lanterns. The handkerchiefs did little to stop the stench of rotten flesh that assaulted us. I gagged, and Mother turned slightly green. The smell in the barn took me back to the gangrene cases in the hospitals on the front, and the floor felt unsteady under my feet.

Sheriff Moore and old Sister Farnsworth stood by an ice-packed body laid out on a make-shift table.

The sheriff grimaced. "Sorry you ladies have to see this, but we're going to want to get him buried quickly. The ice doesn't help much at this stage."

"That's the prospector?" The handkerchief muffled my voice.

"Yep. One of the men who found him recognized his clothes. Scavengers had a go at him, but there's enough left for a respectable burial."

"He didn't die of natural causes," Mother said, coming to stand next to the sheriff, the handkerchief tied over her mouth and nose.

"No, he was shot. Just like Roy. Might have even been the same weapon."

I looked up. "He didn't kill Roy, then."

"No way he could have. He's been dead at least a week by the looks of him." Sheriff Moore glanced at the body and then away to the safety of the shadows. "We took some pictures, but I don't think he's going to tell us anything else. I'll leave you good sisters to your work."

The sheriff started to walk away, but Mother called out to him.

"What was his name?"

Sheriff Moore looked back. "Vern," he said quietly.

Mother nodded, and we all glanced at each other. Vern. He had a name. He died far from home and kin, but at one time he must have been loved by someone. This last act of service was the proper thing to do for him.

We went to work automatically. All of us had prepared bodies before, washing and wrapping and dressing them, in this case in someone's donated suit.

Vern had been shot in the chest. Not like Roy. Had he seen it coming? The same person might have shot both of them. Maybe because of the same secret? Money was a powerful motivation, and Vern had been looking for gold. Most of the locals had poked around the hills at one time or another, but no one ever found more than a little gold dust. Striking gold when people were losing their farms and ranches, though—that would offer temptation.

If only Roy had shared more information in his letter! I looked at Vern's shrouded face and shivered. If two people had died over a secret, there was nothing to stop the murderer from striking again. I ought to be happy I didn't know more. Yet, I was afraid Vern's ghost would haunt me, too, if Roy's message was at the heart of it all and I had failed him.

Vern died first. Maybe Roy found out about it and got scared he was next?

"Where was he found?" I asked quietly.

Sister Brown shrugged. "I'm not sure. Out in the canyons?"

"Does the sheriff think that's where he died?"

"I suppose so. He said he found the bullet. He's going to try to match it with the one that killed Roy."

Then we'd have a good idea if the same person killed him. But it didn't sound like the killer cared much about covering his—or her—tracks regarding the murders. This killer had a different secret to hide. Gold, or something else? I couldn't guess what Roy and Vern had in common, but I suspected a certain pilot might have some clues about Roy.

CHAPTER EIGHT

Victor took his biplane out early the next morning, so I had to wait for my chance to question him. In the meantime, I cut strawberries for breakfast and poured fresh cream over them to serve beside the scrambled eggs and jamón.

Javi and Papa ate quickly. They had weeding to do before it got too hot.

"Coyotes killed a calf last night," Papa said.

"You think it's the same ones that got the Chamberlain's sheep last week?" Javi asked.

"Probably. Once a coyote learns to kill livestock, it becomes dangerous."

They finished breakfast, and Papa took the gun when they left.

I had just tasted my first bite of smoky-sweet jamón when Javi burst in.

"Ten, you'd better come."

He ran back out. I set down my fork and hurried after him. Papa was in the yard talking to LeVon Banks. They watched me approach.

"What is it?" I asked. My mouth had gone dry.

"It's Virginia Hamblin," Papa said softly.

My breath caught. "She's been shot, too?"

LeVon shook his head. "Sheriff brought her in for questioning. Thinks she shot Roy and that prospector."

"Ginny? No! Why would he say that?"

"They were shot with a 3030 Winchester. Like Ginny has."

I gestured to Papa's gun. "We have one, too. Half of Kane County has a 3030."

"There's more," LeVon said, his voice weighty with gossip gathered driving all over the county. "Sheriff found a letter to Miss Hamblin asking her to meet and talk over something. Matches the handwriting on another note of Roy's that the sheriff has."

My skin went cold. "It does?"

"Yep." LeVon scratched his white stubble. "Sheriff figures Roy found out about some secret of hers, and when he went to confront or blackmail her about it, she shot him."

"Oh, no, no, no."

Father put a steadying hand on my arm. LeVon didn't know I was Miss Grace. He didn't know it was my fault the sheriff had that letter.

"There has to be a mistake," I whispered. "The secret has to be about something else. Gold, maybe. The prospector."

LeVon gave me a strange look. "Beats me. Just repeating what I heard."

I looked up at Papa. "I have to go see Ginny."

He nodded.

I started up the Model T. The hand crank slipped and slammed into my arm. I hissed in pain, lucky it hadn't broken the bone. Cradling my bruised arm, I climbed into the car. I watched the pale blue sky for Victor's plane as I drove to Kanab. There weren't many places within flying distance, so where had he gone?

I parked at the sheriff's office and hurried inside, ignoring stares from curious bystanders probably looking for gossip about Ginny's arrest. Sheriff Moore hunched at his desk, his hair ruffled until it stood on end like a startled cat's. Telegrams and papers cluttered the desk. He grimaced when he saw me.

"I assume you're here about your friend?"

I took the seat across from him. "Ginny couldn't have shot anyone."

He held up his hands in a helpless gesture. "I hope she didn't, but I have to follow the evidence, and it's not looking good for her right now."

"Can I see the letter? The new one?"

"You snooping for your old friend Barry?" The sheriff shook his head. "I need to keep the details from the public while I'm still investigating. But you can tell him that we're testing her gun to see if the bullets match the ones found with the bodies."

I didn't want Barry to write anything in the paper about Ginny being under suspicion, though they probably knew all the way up to Long Valley by now. "Is she under arrest?"

"Not yet."

"Can I speak to her?"

He gave me a level stare then nodded once. "Maybe you can talk some sense into her. She's not cooperating, and that's not going to help her case."

He showed me to a plain, uncarpeted room where Ginny sat at a table. Her blond hair was slightly disheveled, and red dirt dusted the knees of her overalls, but she still carried herself like a debutante who had mistakenly wandered into the Kanab jail from Los Angeles or Manhattan. She shut the fashion pages of the Sears Catalog in front of her and glared at the sheriff until he left us alone.

Her bravado faded once the door clicked shut. "Oh, Tenny, what a mess!"

I sat beside her. "I know you didn't do it. We'll prove you're innocent."

"They think I shot a man I've never seen before in my life." She nervously flipped her thumb over the edge of the catalog. "Said they found him not far from my property. And my gun has been fired recently. Of course, it has! I was shooting at jackrabbits. Can't keep them out of my crops."

She had worried the edge of the catalog until it frayed, so I grabbed her hand. "It's going to be all right. We just have to find out who *did* shoot Roy and Vern."

"Is that the other fellow's name?" Her voice was tired.

I nodded.

"Poor man."

"Is there any chance Roy had a connection to him?"

"Sure. I don't know who Roy associated with. I'm starting to wish I'd been a bit nosier." She smiled grimly.

"Do you think Roy ever snuck off to look for gold, too?"

She looked up at the plastered ceiling. "Maybe. Sam sometimes mentioned that Roy wasn't always where he said he'd be."

"Why did you keep him around if he wasn't reliable?"

"He got his work done eventually. And it can be hard to find men who are willing to work for a woman and treat her like the boss."

"He was always respectful?"

"At least he acted like I was the one in charge. I think he was grateful for the work."

"Did he say anything about where he came from?"

"Up north somewhere. I didn't need to ask a lot of questions as long as he could work with the cattle. I have a feeling not many people were willing to give him a chance."

"You were."

"Sometimes all we need is a chance." She met my eyes. "If you're able to find anything out about who shot him, I'd be grateful. Not just because it would get me out of here. Roy wasn't a bad guy. He didn't deserve that."

It sounded like Ginny didn't know what he deserved, but I supposed people did deserve a second chance. Sometimes the past was hard to get away from, though.

"Have you heard anything about this pilot who's come to town?" I asked. "Victor Holbrook?"

"Doesn't sound familiar. Why?"

"I think he knew Roy, or his name, at least. He looked startled when I said that Roy was dead."

"He probably didn't kill him then."

"But he might know something about Roy. About his secrets."

"Oh, you mean that blasted letter."

"You saw it?"

"Only when the sheriff showed it to me. I'd never seen either of them before."

"The one addressed to you?"

Ginny shook her head. "I never received it, and I've got no idea what it's about. I have to guess Roy found out about something unsavory going on and he was going to tell me, but we'll never know now what it was."

"Yes, we will," I said.

Ginny raised an eyebrow.

"At least one other person knows his secret," I said.

"Someone who's willing to kill over it, you mean. Not wise, Tenny."

I stared off into the corner and imagined the faces of dead soldiers staring back at me. "I'm tired of being helpless. Watching innocent people suffer."

Ginny leaned forward. "Look, I'll tell the sheriff what I know about Roy. You tell him about this pilot. I think Sheriff's a thick-headed cuss for arresting me, but I don't want anyone else to get hurt."

I nodded reluctantly. Ginny squeezed my hand, and I headed for the door.

The sheriff was waiting outside, and by his smug expression, I guessed he'd been eavesdropping.

"I suppose you already heard," I said, "but I think the pilot, Victor Holbrook, knows something about Roy."

"Thank you, ma'am. I'll keep that in mind."

He tipped his hat and went back in to talk to Ginny. I wandered across the street to Barry Hansen's. Myrtle invited me in.

"I have some more letters for you," Barry told me. "I kept the envelopes this time. In case."

I nodded, feeling queasy. If I had done something about the Trouble in Boots letter sooner, maybe Roy would be alive and Ginny wouldn't be under suspicion. And if I hadn't turned the letter over to the sheriff, they would have less reason to suspect her. I accepted the new letters and tucked them into my purse, hoping they wouldn't have any more pleas for help that I couldn't answer.

"Is the newspaper running an obituary for Roy?" I asked

"The first guy who was shot?"

"Yeah, that's him."

"We'll put in a death notice, but nobody knows him well enough to write an obituary."

"Nobody knows anything about him?"

"Hardly anybody even heard of him before he got shot."

"Is he going to be buried here?"

"I suppose if nobody else wants him."

"There's no word that anyone's missing him?" It was sad, and possibly suspicious. Was he hiding from someone?

"You're worried about Virginia Hamblin's role in all this?"

I nodded. "You're not putting anything about her in the paper, are you?"

"Just that the body was found on her property. For now, that's all there is to tell." Barry pursed his lips. "Your idea about an obituary isn't a bad one. I'll see if I can find anything about him from editors up north. If I run a short bit on him, maybe it'll drum up some more information."

"Thank you!"

He shrugged. "Just... if things do come down on the wrong side for Virginia Hamblin, I'll have to report that, too."

"That won't happen."

He and Myrtle exchanged a worried look and waved goodbye as I exited the print shop. The distant buzz of a plane froze me in my tracks. I took a deep breath and forced myself to relax. I couldn't run from Victor and his plane. In fact, I had to chase him down.

CHAPTER NINE

Victor came back too late for me to corner him without making it look like I had something scandalous in mind.

The next morning, his plane waited in the pasture near a few cows that were brave enough to venture near their strange mechanical bedfellow, but there was no sign of the pilot.

I cleaned up after breakfast and helped Rosie weed until the heat sent us scrambling for shade and cool water. Ginny could be home now, and Sam or the other ranch hands might tell me more about Roy. I took my bike and walked it through the deep sand toward the road.

"Hey-ya, Doll! Where you off to?"

I did not disguise my eye roll as I looked back at Victor. "Excuse me?"

"I wondered where you were going."

"I got that part. My name isn't Doll."

"Babe? Honey-bunch? Sweetheart?" He waggled his eyebrows and grinned. "Am I getting warmer?"

"Colder every minute." I turned my back on him and walked on.

He kept pace with me. "Come on, I'm trying to be friendly."

"Parking your noisy airplane in someone's field is not the best way to make friends."

He shrugged and wrinkled his eyes against the sun. "I've made friends all over the country this way."

"Oh, I'm sure you have."

He chuckled. "I didn't mean it like that. I've never been much of a ladies' man. Don't know how to talk to the fairer sex."

"You don't say."

"It's hard to believe, isn't it?" He smiled and held out his hand. "Come on, let's try to be friends?"

I shook my head. "You're just in town for your flying circus and then you'll be off again."

"Does that mean you'll miss me when I'm gone?"

"Get going and I'll let you know."

He laughed. "See, I *can* talk to you. You keep things lively. Speaking of which, are you the one who ratted me out to the sheriff?"

"Ratted you out?"

"Told him I knew Roy Shelton." He held up his hands to show fingers stained charcoal grey. "He even took my fingerprints. How do you like that?"

"*Did* you know him?"

He shrugged. "The name's familiar, and I meet a lot of people. What did he look like?"

I studying him, trying to decide if he was telling the truth. "I never met him." I picked up my pace, and Victor loped through the sand to keep up.

"So, where are we off to?"

"You can't come."

"Why not? Is it a ladies' book club or something? I bet they'll let me join the party. Oh, it's not a date, is it? Because it would be very ungallant of the gentleman to make you ride your bike to meet him."

"It's none of your business."

"But I'm bored. I hate being bored."

"That's none of *my* business."

"Maybe you're right. I've always wanted to try to rope a cow."

I stopped and glared at him.

"Is it true that you can tip them over?" He studied the cows with mock seriousness.

"You wouldn't."

He wandered over to the fence and lifted his cap to scratch his head. "They seem pretty heavy. Is tipping them a two-person job?"

"You'll hurt them! Is everything a game to you?"

His expression turned serious. "I'm not trying to hurt anyone. I just... I feel like I always need to be moving, doing. I tried to help with the corn, but your father wouldn't let me." He gave me a beseeching look. "Come on, whatever errand you're on, certainly I can help."

"Have you thought about looking for gold?" Maybe that's what really brought him to the desert. I watched his reaction carefully.

His forehead wrinkled. "Is that what you folks do for fun? No, thanks. I'd rather enjoy that big, empty desert of yours from above. Those canyons look awfully lonely."

I studied him. And the poor cow. If Victor knew Roy Shelton— knew something about what happened to him—he might steer me in the wrong direction. On the other hand, if he was with me, I could watch how he reacted to everyone. And keep him from bothering the cows.

"I'm going to visit my neighbor," I said. "I suppose you may accompany me."

"Thank you! I'll try to be on my best behavior."

"I should hope so." I left my bike leaning against a fence post and resigned myself to walking. "We may be out in the country, but we're not a bunch of rubes. People often get the wrong idea about Utah."

"Don't I know it. I'm a native son."

"What?"

"Yep, I was born in Provo. My ancestors pulled their handcarts across the plains, and Gramps did a stint in the state pen for polygamy. Can you get any more Utah than that?" He practically crowed over it. Like the people at church who acted like because they had settled a place first, it belonged to them and no one else.

"You're not the only one with pioneer ancestors."

"Were you born here, then? I mean, your father…"

"I'm from Colonia Juarez, but Papa's people have known the West longer than any of your—or my—handcart-pulling ancestors."

"No need to get defensive. I'm not trying to take anything away from him."

I shrugged. People always acted like Spaniards and Mexicans didn't belong in the West. And when Utah had been part of Mexico first. Mother's stories about her people suffering and struggling to cross the plains, following their beliefs, inspired me to keep going when things were hard. Abuela, too, moving from Spain to Mexico to Utah, willing to start over again and again. But though I'd never met Papa's father, something about his people spoke to me as well: that uneasy blend of Spanish and Indian that survived by intense family loyalty and pride in wrestling a livelihood from the often-unkind lands of the West.

Victor didn't say much else until we reached the gate posts at the bottom of the lane leading up to Ginny's place.

"So, is this fellow a pretty good friend?"

"Yes, she is."

He gave me a lopsided grin when I said "she," but I pretended not to notice.

We neared the bunkhouse, which was roped off.

"What happened here?" Victor asked. He seemed sincerely curious, but he might be a good actor.

"That's where Roy Shelton was shot."

His eyes widened, and he looked back at the bunkhouse, his gaze speculative. "I heard they were questioning a woman about the shooting. So, your friend—"

"She didn't shoot anyone."

His eyes brightened. "You want to clear your friend's name! What kind of clues are we looking for?"

"We're not looking for clues. I just… I want to hear more about what happened. About Roy."

Victor was quiet for a few steps. "Did you ever think that knowing more about him might be dangerous? Some secrets, it's better to steer clear of."

I shot him a sharp look. Was he warning me? Or threatening me? "I'm going to help my friend."

He frowned thoughtfully then gave a decisive nod. "All right, Sherlock. I'll be your Watson."

"I didn't ask you to."

He winked. "I'm just a helpful sort." He met my eyes, all joking gone. "Besides, if I knew this fellow, I'd like to find out what happened to him."

He watched me, looking both determined and anxious that I agree. But I couldn't be sure his motives were honest.

"Hey, what are you doing here?"

We both jerked around to see a dark-haired man in jeans and a ten-gallon hat striding up.

"No tourists!" He made a shooing motion. "You're trespassing."

I stepped forward. "I'm Tenny Mateo, from up the road. I'm here to check on Ginny."

The man squinted at me, highlighting his deep tan and the wrinkles around his eyes. "Mateo? Are you related to Feliciana Ruiz de Mateo?"

When he said the name, I heard the traces of his Spanish accent. "Sí. She's my abuela."

His face broke out in a bright grin. "Casimiro says she makes the best croquetas in America. I haven't had a good croqueta since I was a kid."

I smiled. "You should come to the house sometime. She loves guests who appreciate her food."

And I didn't mind a reason for her to cook croquetas. Dough made with flour and milk, maybe some chopped jamón or cheese, then breaded and fried. My mouth watered at the thought.

He nodded. "I'm Ramón. You said you're looking for Miss Hamblin?"

"I wanted to see how she's doing. Did they let her come home?"

"Late last night." He glanced back at the house. "She's out checking on the cattle. Mad as a hornet. We've all been trying to keep our distance."

"At least she's not in jail," I said.

"*Sí*. She's a good employer. I don't think she shot Roy. She had no reason."

"Did you know him well?"

"Not really. He kept to himself. He seemed a little lazy, but otherwise all right." Ramón glanced over his shoulder and said in a quieter voice. "Sam hated him, though."

"Sam Ellis?"

"Yes. He didn't show it much, but if he ever looked at me the way he looked at Roy, I'd be worried for my job."

"But not your life?" Victor asked.

I glared at Victor, but Ramón looked thoughtful. "I've never seen Sam lose his temper, and he doesn't want to see the boss in trouble. I think he'd confess before he'd let that happen, even if he didn't do it."

I nodded. "Tell Ginny I stopped by. And come visit Abuela sometime."

"Will do." He smiled.

I turned to walk back down the lane. Ramón was right. Sam did seem to have a cool head on his shoulders. So, if he had a reason to hate Roy, less cool-headed people probably did, too.

Victor walked slowly, his brow furrowed in thought. I gave him a questioning look, waiting for the dazzling insight he would offer about Roy.

"I think," he said slowly, "I need to hear more about these croquetas."

CHAPTER TEN

That afternoon, I sat at the secretary desk to answer the newest Miss Grace letters, inhaling the faint scent of the Murphy's Oil Soap that Mother used to polish the wood. The buzz of Victor's biplane intruded on my quiet. Each time it drew close, I froze, letters forgotten, waiting to hear the ghosts of screams.

But this wasn't the Great War. It was Kane County with its simpler problems. I was safe here. At least, I was supposed to be, when killers weren't wandering the canyons. I picked up a small piece of petrified wood I'd found in a dry wash and turned it over in my fingers, the stone ridges unyielding even when I squeezed. Focus on the letters.

A question about clearing up freckles. Mother would know more about that, with her Gaelic skin. How to grow bigger roses. Ha! I would be helping my competition at the fair, but I could afford to share some tips.

The next letter kept my attention, and I set down the petrified wood.

Dear Miss Grace,

I think my neighbor is making moonshine. I hate to be a Mrs. Grundy, but isn't that dangerous?

So, Kane County had a bootlegger? I wasn't surprised. And the informer was a man, by the looks of his handwriting. Maybe he hoped to tattle on his criminal neighbor without getting involved himself. Well, I would help him and throw in some tidbits about the dangers of moonshine for good measure. Just a few months earlier, a bad batch of the stuff had killed dozens of people back east and blinded many more.

As I scratched out my response, the biplane skimmed right over the house. I flinched and put down my pen with a huff, ready to give Victor a dressing down that would make a drill sergeant proud.

I stepped out into the bright sun. Model Ts, wagons, and bikes cluttered the dirt lane leading to our yard. Men in caps or Stetsons and women in cloche hats gathered outside the house, craning to watch the biplane dip and soar over the countryside. I gaped. When had our homestead become a circus?

Javi ran up to me. "Isn't this great? People came all the way from Orderville and Fredonia, and this is just the first day."

"The *first* day?" I asked.

"The first day of plane rides. People are paying ten dollars each, and we get a cut!"

Ten dollars! It would help the farm. Which was good, since some of the crowd wandered through our fields and trampled the squash plants I had just weeded the week before.

"Victor gave Barry Hansen a free ride so he'd write it up in the paper," Javi said. "People are going to come from all over. I got a free ride, too. You should try it! It's amazing. I wish I could have been a pilot in the war."

I turned on Javi. "Don't say things like that! Do you realize how many aviators died during the war? And stunt pilots crash all the time."

"Victor must be really good to have survived, then."

"Or lucky." So much of it was luck.

"Why do you hate him so much?" Javi sounded hurt.

I shrugged and rubbed my arms. "I just don't trust him."

Victor buzzed low over the cattle, stampeding them across the sagebrush-studded range, before landing to switch out passengers for another circle over the canyons.

I made my way over to Barry Hansen, who jotted notes on his writing pad.

"Hi, Tenny!" he said with a quick glance up. "Isn't this amazing? The power of flight. It's exhilarating."

"It sounds like your coverage is going to generate more business."

"Nothing for your family to complain about, that's for sure."

I nodded. "And I can have my letters to you before you go, if it quiets down enough for me to finish."

"Excellent! I heard some news that might interest you."

"About Ginny?"

"Yup. Well, about Roy. I telegraphed some of my editor friends up north. I found out what he was running away from."

"Oh?"

"He was one of the Wobblies."

"The... Oh, the Industrial Workers of the World." Reds. Communists. Anarchists. "Hmm."

"'Hmm' is right."

"You think his past caught up with him."

"I think it gives the sheriff something to look at besides Virginia Hamblin's gun."

I considered that. "Are you going to print anything about Roy being a Wobbly?"

"Of course."

"Is that wise? There have been riots back east. How are people going to react if they think communists are killing people in Kane County?"

"You know any Reds?"

"No." But to many people, "anarchist" was a synonym for Southern European immigrant: Italian. Greek. Maybe Spanish?

"Neither do I. If there are any Reds sneaking around murdering people, the paper needs to warn everyone to be on their guard. No one will panic. We're not like the city folks back east." He held up his pencil and pad. "Besides, it's our job to tell the truth."

I frowned at that. It was hard to tell the truth when you weren't sure what it was.

Nobody else knew either, based on the snatches of gossip drifting around me.

"Can you believe about Virginia Hamblin?"

"Well, we all remember what her father was like."

"That Indian knows more than he's letting on."

"Bo Young is sure anxious to get his hands on her land."

And speaking of the devil, Bo Young had elbowed his way past other people wanting a flight, dragging his son Mel behind him.

When Victor strolled over to find his next passenger, Bo thrust twenty dollars at him. A lot of money for a struggling homesteader.

"A ride for me, and one for my son," Bo said, the smugness on his ruddy face making him look even more like a tom turkey.

"I'm not going, sir." Mel pushed up the spectacles that held his tin mask in place and shot an apologetic glance at the people his father had pushed aside to reach the front.

"Don't be a coward, boy!"

Victor and I both winced, and our eyes met, a flash of understanding passing between us. Whatever else Victor was, he had been in the war, too. He knew.

Mel's face reddened behind his mask.

"Sorry, Sir," Victor said with exaggerated politeness. "I only have enough gasoline for one more flight today."

"Oh, fine. Just take me over the Hamblin property, then, so I can get a good look at all that land that's going to be mine someday." Bo chuckled like he expected everyone to laugh along. No one did. Mel looked down and scuffed the toe of his boot in the dirt.

Once Bo was settled into the cockpit and the biplane bounced down the field and took off, Mel turned to me. "I'm sorry about my father. I know Sister Hamblin is a friend of yours."

I shrugged. "We all know your dad wants that property. At least he doesn't make a secret out of it."

Mel's forehead furrowed. "I suppose." He sounded like he wanted to say more.

Did Mel know something about his father and Ginny? Bo Young wanted that land badly. Could he have hired Roy to cause trouble, knowing Ginny had a soft spot for hiring tramps? That *would* be a dangerous secret.

I didn't want to be too obvious, so my conversation with Mel was only enough to get some distracted responses about his family's homestead before the plane circled back into view and touched down in the field, sending a cloud of red dust into the blue sky.

Bo strutted off with Mel in tow. The onlookers hurried past me to gawk at the parked biplane. Victor strolled over, keeping one eye on the crowd around his plane, and tilted his head after Bo.

"He's a piece of work, isn't he?"

"Did he really want to look over the Hamblin place?"

"Twice. Like he was searching for something, actually." He arched his eyebrows. "Would you like to take a gander as well? Things can seem different from up there."

I folded my arms. "I don't have ten dollars to spare."

"Don't be silly. Your family flies for free." He pulled a mock grimace. "Except your grandmother. I offered, and she stuck her finger in my face and said some things in Spanish that I doubt were fit for polite company."

I chuckled. Abuela would not trust a flying machine.

Could I learn anything from the perspective Victor offered? At this point, I wasn't sure what I was looking for, but I doubted Bo Young was just sightseeing when he flew over the Hamblin place. Yet Ginny's property struggled more than the Youngs' and ours. Not enough water. Her homestead would offer Bo more grazing land, but that was all I could think of.

LeVon Banks popped up next to Victor. "You're doing very well here, son, but I have some ideas that might increase your profits. What you ought to be doing is charging one buck to go up."

"One dollar! It wouldn't even cover my fuel."

LeVon grinned, flashing his gold tooth. "Then charge 'em ten to bring 'em back down. Or even twenty! They'll pay! Do some loop-the-loops if they don't."

"Clever," Victor said with the smile he used when he was more annoyed than amused. "I would like them to actually enjoy the ride, though."

LeVon rubbed his white-stubbled chin. "Maybe I'll use that one myself. Ten cents gets you a tour out to the canyons. Fifty cents gets you back to Kanab. And for a dollar, I'll avoid the rattlers and the big, hairy spiders." He slapped his knee and laughed. "Bo will like that one. Where'd he go?"

Victor shook his head as LeVon wandered off, then he returned his challenging gaze to meet my defiant one. "Well? Are you going to fly?"

"Fine," I said. "Tomorrow morning."

After that, I wanted to pay a visit to Sam Ellis to see why he hated the dead man.

AFTER EVERYONE else had turned in for the night, I sat up by the light of a single kerosene lamp, the warm scent of burning oil keeping me company as I stitched a torn seam on a skirt. Between the Miss Grace letters and plane rides and worrying about Ginny, I'd fallen behind on my usual chores. Daisy sprawled out on the rug, tongue lolling out of her mouth. Our thick adobe walls kept some of the heat out during the day, but it still took several hours for the chilly night air of the desert to cool off the house.

Daisy's head perked up, fixed on the kitchen, and a growl rumbled in her throat.

"What is it, girl?" I stood, staring into the dark kitchen.

Daisy barked and ran to the kitchen door. I grabbed the rifle and followed her to peer out the window. Nothing moved in the dim light from the waning moon. But Victor was sleeping in the barn, and his plane was out there. We were far enough from town that it should have been safe from anyone prowling around, but there might have been some curious kids sneaking about.

I put my hand on the doorknob and paused. There was also a killer on the loose. An anarchist? They wouldn't find much to sabotage on our farm. Unless they wanted to damage Victor's plane.

Or they could be murdering Victor right now because of whatever he knew about Roy.

I yanked the door open. Daisy shot out, barking wildly. I lifted the rifle.

"Mr. Holbrook?" I asked.

No response. Daisy kept up her frantic barks, running circles around the yard and earning some disgruntled clucks from the chicken coop. The dog wouldn't carry on like that at Victor anymore, would she?

I stepped out into the cool air, rifle up, listening for anything besides Daisy and the occasional chirp of a cricket. A scorpion darted across my foot, and I gasped and almost pulled the trigger.

A shadowy figure shambled in the darkness near the plane. My first thought was ghosts dragged back from the Western Front by the biplane like seaweed tangled on an oar, but I shook my head. The Jenny was only used for training. Stateside. Was Victor sleepwalking or drunk? "Mr. Holbrook!"

"Miss Mateo?" His voice came from the barn.

I spun to see him striding up to me. I wasn't one of those silly, fainting girls—not after the war—but I wanted to hide behind his reassuring presence as I pointed.

"There's someone over there," I whispered. "Maybe drunk."

Victor's brow furrowed. He nodded and crept forward. I followed behind with the rifle pointed up. The figure stumbled back into view, falling onto his hands and knees.

"Not a threat," Victor whispered.

I moved my finger away from the trigger. We walked up to the figure, who was now curled up in a ball on the ground. Mel Young.

"Mel?" I knelt beside him. The stench of sweat and alcohol filled the night air. "What happened?"

"I need to ride the plane," he slurred. "Not a coward."

"Of course, you're not," I said.

"Sister Mateo?" He groaned and put his hands over his tin mask. "You shouldn't see me like this."

Victor rolled him over gently. "You've been partaking of liquid courage."

"Don't tell anyone," Mel pleaded.

"We won't," Victor said. "But if you got your hands on some moonshine, you've got to be careful. It can be stronger than you think. Poison, even."

"I know. I know I shouldn't be drinking. Don't tell my Pa. He'll kill me."

Victor hauled him into a sitting position. "We'll sober you up and get you home."

"I'm such a failure."

"Nah, you're just having a rough day. I've got you." Victor nodded to me, and I backed off. Victor probably knew better than I did how to handle a drunk man. Not that I hadn't seen it on the front, but Mel wouldn't want a neighbor to see him struggling. We all had to keep our demons hidden, put on a brave face. Mel wasn't the only one wearing a mask after the war.

I went back in to find Papa standing in the kitchen. Daisy ran past us to the living room. Papa glanced at the rifle. I put it back in its place.

"Just some kids wanting to see the plane," I said.

Papa nodded and locked the door again. I felt badly about lying to him, but I would have felt like a traitor telling the truth.

CHAPTER ELEVEN

The next morning, under the pretense of cleaning the living room, I pulled open the secretary desk and stared at the letter about the moonshiner. Written by a man. Mel's misery hovered in my mind's eye. He must know the moonshiner.

"Miss Mateo?" Victor's voice interrupted.

I jumped and covered the Miss Grace letters with blank paper. He raised an eyebrow, but I rose and put my back to the desk.

"You ready for that airplane ride?" he asked.

"Of course." I shut the letters inside the fold-up desk.

Victor held the door for me, glancing at the desk before following me out. He couldn't know about Miss Grace, could he? Even if he did, it didn't seem like his style to tell people it was me.

Out in the alfalfa-scented green of the pasture, Victor started the propeller to warm up the biplane engine. The breeze from the blades whipped my hair, and I flinched at the sound.

Victor watched me thoughtfully, but he didn't tease or ask invasive questions. Instead, he offered a hand. I took it tentatively, surprised to find his grip both gentle and strong.

"Here, let me show you the controls." He helped me step onto the wing and gestured to the rear cockpit. "The cable by my feet controls the rudder, this is the stick, telegraph transmitter, and the instruments that tell me RPMs, air speed, things like that."

"Easier than driving the Model T," I said with a nervous laugh.

"You bet. You'll keep an eye on the fuel for me," he pointed to the gauge in front of the forward seat. "We can stay up longer than fifteen minutes for this flight." He patted the fabric skin of the plane. "She's got a ninety-horsepower engine, can go over seventy miles per hour. Not as good as the Sopwith Camels we flew overseas, but she was a good trainer."

He helped me into the front cockpit and handed me a flight cap. It would keep my hair from getting tangled, but if we crashed, a bit of leather wasn't going to save my head. The vibration of the engine hummed through me, softened some of my fear into excitement.

"You ready?" he asked.

I nodded, then realized he might not be able to see me that well from the ground, with the little windshield in front of me. "Yes."

He yanked away the blocks in front of the wheels and clambered around the wing cables to scurry into the rear cockpit. The engine picked up, and the plane eased forward. The wind whistled over the grind of the propeller, and we bounced over the rough pasture. Faster and faster.

And then the field slowly sunk beneath us. I gasped and held on to the edge of the cockpit. The green alfalfa dropped farther below, and we banked to the side. Below us, Papa's homestead spread out, magnificent in the morning light, a strange mixture of straight, neat rows of green and the wildness of the Utah desert. The cattle milled about like lazy ants. This would be a fantastic way to round them up in the fall.

We turned northeast, sailing over the Pahreah River. I gasped at the colors. The stripes of red, orange, purple, white, and green were always my favorite, but at this angle, they looked even more magnificent, the colors wrapping around the mountains as if painted on by God.

I leaned over, trying to decide where we were. There was the road. I traced down past our homestead to Ginny's property. Even from this distance, the difference between her homestead and ours struck me. The only green on her land was the dusky freckles of juniper on the red-blushed hills. With her branch of the stream dry, the desert quickly reclaimed its own.

Victor turned southwest, taking us over the Young property. Like ours, his had stretches of green with plenty of cattle. It was hard to tell, but it seemed that he had more animals than we did. He might have been grazing them in the Kaibab Forest on the strip between the Arizona border and the Grand Canyon, but even then, the range was too dry and overrun by deer to be much good to cattle.

"Anything else you want to see?" Victor shouted at me over the sound of the engine.

"More of the canyons."

He obliged, and we soared north again, this time going higher and farther into the desert, beyond even where the sheep and their shepherds wandered. The Pahreah River snaked down from the canyons, an artery of life in the barren red. Then we left it behind. The peaks of the hills ran over the landscape like veins. Juniper trees dotted the ground with their deep blue-green.

From above, the lines of color on the cliffs reminded me of the tree rings in my petrified wood, each one holding stories and secrets of the past. We lived in the lap of the desert, but it was not a nurturing mother. A distant goddess, perhaps, like those worshipped by Papa's Native ancestors far before the Spanish arrived: tolerating us for the moment, or perhaps simply not awakened to our presence yet. She did not love us, did not know us, and in a way, we could never fully know her, no matter how we loved her.

I glanced at the fuel gauge. One-quarter full.

"We should head back," I called to Victor.

The plane banked south, returning to the course of the river. Pahreah's struggling town site appeared beneath us, followed by the homesteads. If only the desert could tell us her secrets. What secret had Vern discovered? What would Roy have told Ginny if he'd had the chance to speak to her? Was a rich gold vein hidden in the canyons? Perhaps Bo had contrived something to get Ginny off her homestead so she couldn't prove up. Or an anarchist lurked among us, ready to strike a devastating blow to southern Utah's economy. We could not withstand another disaster.

And Victor. I pictured the way he had taken my hand, the understanding in his eyes. He was not the shallow braggart I had taken him for, but he was still hiding something.

Our homestead spread out again to welcome me back. The ground rushed up at us, but we bounced into the landing with only a minor jolt, and Victor slowed the plane to a stop.

"You handled that very well," he said as he helped me out of the cockpit. "No fear of heights."

I stumbled against his chest while climbing off the wing, and heat prickled over my cheeks. He steadied me, not moving or speaking. I inhaled the warm scent of leather and wanted to linger. It was deceptively peaceful with his arms bracing me, a moment that seemed to stretch on, but when it ended, things would get complicated. I forced myself to find my feet.

"Heights don't bother me," I said quickly, then added more softly, "It felt very free."

He watched me for a moment. "You were a nurse, I bet."

"What?"

"In the war."

I nodded.

"Rough job. But necessary. Not that pilots often left enough behind to be nursed." I frowned, and he added quickly, "I'm sorry. Gallows humor."

"I know." I did understand, but I'd never gotten used to it, despite the number of soldiers and even doctors and nurses who used it to deflect the constant fear and tension.

"Nothing flaps you, I suppose. You're one of those noble women bandaging wounds while the shells fall around you."

No. As the shells fell around me, I'd huddled in the dark with dying men and prayed we would not be hit. I had frozen. If I held still, I could get hit. If I moved, I could get hit. No matter what I did—

"Tenny?" Victor's voice broke through the memories.

I stared at him.

"I'm sorry," he said, his eyes full of painful understanding.

I nodded curtly and hurried back in the house.

CHAPTER TWELVE

I needed to get back to Ginny's, but for the rest of the week, our homestead was overrun with our "customers," as Mother had taken to calling them—even the ones who just came to gawk. At first, she tried to keep them supplied with lemonade but, after Ramón stopped by to take a peek at the plane and implore Abuela for croquetas, we were handing out those as well.

"Are there more of those dough things?" neighbors and strangers called to me as they waited for airplane rides.

When I wasn't working in the kitchen with Abuela, I fought to keep the "customers" out of our crops. After all, Victor would be gone soon, and we still had to survive.

I woke Saturday morning with feet still aching from running around the Friday afternoon crowd and with lingering dreams of frying dough swimming in my head. Forget about "flying circus," the airshow promised to be a regular circus, complete with runaway lions and flaming tents. Perhaps flaming lions. I shook my head and sat up in the pre-dawn grayness. I would steal the early morning back, at least, before the hordes of "customers" devoured the rest of my day.

I snuck out the front door and pedaled my bike up the road to Ginny's homestead. Other than Ramón, I hadn't seen any of Ginny's people at our place. I didn't blame her for staying away from the crowds.

Only the occasional mooing of a scruffy cow with the rocking boot brand broke the morning quiet. Sam sat on the porch of the bunkhouse, an unconscious Paiute man with a grey tinge to his skin curled up on a cot next to him. Sam nodded a greeting to me. His eyes were tired and wary.

"What happened?" I asked, motioning to his companion.

He hesitated like he was trying to decide if he trusted me. Finally, he shrugged.

"Alcohol poisoning. Got ahold of some bad moonshine." Sam's voice carried a mix of anger and sadness. "Marshal Little was going to arrest him, probably let him die in a jail cell, so I brought him here to try to nurse him through it."

"Poor man."

"Poor stupid man." Sam shook his head. "Addiction is a powerful demon."

"Where does he get the alcohol?" I asked, remembering the Miss Grace letter.

Again, he paused, sizing me up. "Bootleggers sneak it onto the reservation. Feeding the old 'drunk Indian' stereotype. Who cares who it hurts, so long as they make a few bucks?"

I scowled, thinking about Mel. "They must be heartless."

But Barry would circulate the newspaper with the Miss Grace letter about the moonshiner today—he liked to get it out before Sunday, when everyone heard all the news at church—and that might stir up some interest in finding the bootlegger, or at least make the fellow think twice about selling bad moonshine.

"What brings you here?" Sam asked gruffly.

It was my turn to scrutinize him. Could Sam have anything to do with Roy's death? If he did, I doubted he would let Ginny take the blame for it. I chose honesty.

"I'm worried about Ginny. I know she didn't shoot Roy. I want to find out who did, and... well, I heard you were angry with him."

Sam puffed out a breath. "You think you can do better than the sheriff?"

"I hope I can."

"Why?"

"Because... because I don't want to see an innocent person suffer."

"No, I mean, why do you suppose that you can help her?"

I flushed. "Maybe I can't, but I know things they don't."

"Why don't you tell them?"

"I tried. They won't listen. If they won't listen, then what choice do I have?"

His face softened. "Well, we know what it's like to be ignored, don't we? All right. Yeah, I didn't like Roy. I'll show you why." He motioned for me to follow him into the boarding house. "The sheriff has already been through here, but he didn't give much thought to this."

Sam handed me an empty glass jar. I examined it at arm's length then held it closer. A sour stench hit my nose.

"Ugh. It stinks. Moonshine?"

"Looks that way. And he didn't get it from Miss Hamblin's, I can tell you that."

"Hmm." I held it up to the sunlight. It was a typical glass jar, easy to find anywhere. But the liquor wasn't. Roy must have known more people around town than I realized. At least, someone was selling him liquor, and who knows what else they had been up to?

"So, the times when he didn't show up to work, you think he was drunk?" I asked.

"No. I never smelled alcohol on his breath. I would have fired him for that. I suspect he was selling the stuff."

"To the Paiutes?"

"Probably. Or he knew who was."

"He was a bootlegger."

"He had no still to make the moonshine. He must have been a middle man. Maybe for someone local, maybe for someone up north."

"Hmm. There's a letter in the paper today about someone making moonshine." I didn't want to tell him what else I knew: that the writer had been a man. Could Bo Young be the bootlegger and Mel the informant? Was that where Mel got his "liquid courage?" Roy had a dangerous secret. Would someone kill over moonshine? There was money involved, so perhaps.

Sam scowled. "I hope they find the guy that's doing it and lock him up."

"Did Roy ever say anything about his time up north? What he was running away from? The paper claimed he was an anarchist."

"He never said anything about politics or anything else. I got the impression he was just trying to survive."

"Have you met the pilot who's in town, Victor Holbrook?"

Sam pulled off his ten-gallon hat and scratched his head. "Nope. Why?"

"I think he knew Roy." As a communist? As a bootlegger? Neither fit with what I'd seen of Victor.

"You figure he had something to do with the shooting?"

"I don't know," I admitted. "He doesn't seem like a killer, but I don't trust people who keep secrets."

Sam laughed dryly. "You don't have any secrets?"

I considered Miss Grace, and my cheeks warmed. "Well, maybe I do." And from answering the Miss Grace letters, I knew that almost everyone did. Secret fears, secret annoyances, secret weaknesses. What were Sam's secrets? Victor's? Ginny's?

"Why don't you try taking the moonshine jar to the sheriff?" Sam asked. "He might listen to you, especially after it was in the paper."

I nodded. "Thanks for telling me about it. Let me know if you remember anything else."

"Sure. Now, someone keeps knocking down parts of my fence"—he glared toward Bo Young's place—"and I have to fix them before the cattle escape. Mind if I get to work?"

"No, of course not. Thanks for your help. Tell Ginny I stopped by."

He tipped his hat and walked out.

I wrapped the glass jar in a handkerchief and shoved it into my purse, then I biked toward Kanab. My mind churned the whole time. Could the bootlegger be from up north? No one in town had admitted to knowing anything about Roy. But they wouldn't want to admit *how* they knew him if they were buying or selling moonshine.

"Ho, there, Sister Mateo!" LeVon Banks pulled up beside me, scattering a cloud of red dust. "Do you want a ride into town?"

"Thank you!" I put my bike in the back of the Model T truck with the mail and packages, and LeVon moved a couple of telegrams to make room for me on the wide front seat.

I made small talk with LeVon for a few minutes then said, "I was thinking about Kanab. Remember when those women took over the city council?"

He laughed, his gold tooth glinting in the sunlight. "Do I ever. Everyone thought it was a joke, but those ladies took the job seriously."

"They were ahead of their time in clamping down on alcohol."

"Sure were. Checked all the mail to be sure no one was smuggling it in."

"Do you suppose anyone still tries that?"

"What, sending moonshine through the mail? You read the paper already, huh?" He rubbed his stubbly chin. "It's possible. People are clever about making a bit of money on the side. Not a bad idea actually."

I laughed. "You don't check it, then?"

"Not unless someone asks me too. I'm not one to interfere with free trade, though I'd have to turn them in if they tried to mail liquor now."

"You've never caught anyone at it, then?"

"Nah. Most folks here are pretty law abiding. If they are making moonshine, I would guess it's just for themselves."

"Do you suppose it goes on much?" LeVon knew practically everyone in Kane County and had a good memory for all the gossip that came his way.

"Well, I hear of dances every once in a while where some kids have slipped something into the drinks. It wouldn't be hard to make. Your Pa's not the only one who has grape vines on his property, and I see lots of people growing hops along their porch. For decoration, of course."

"Of course." I chuckled.

In the past, Papa had made a mild wine for the Catholics to use in their Mass, but now there was so much competition as vineyards tried to find a legal market for their products, he decided it wasn't worth the trouble of shipping it to Monticello or beyond. What I had smelled in that jar was much stronger than sacramental wine, though. Was there enough demand for moonshine in Kane County for Roy to smuggle it in from elsewhere? Or was someone making it here and sending it out?

"You gonna take up smuggling?" LeVon asked.

I gave an exaggerated sigh. "I would look fetching as a desperado, wouldn't I? If things get bad enough, maybe I'll have to."

His face turned serious. "Now, don't fret. There are always other ways to bring in some cash, even after your pilot friend heads off. You should talk your Pa into trying some of these new cattle I've been telling him about. Bo Young is running some on his property."

"How can he manage food or water for more cattle?" I wondered aloud.

LeVon just shrugged. He parked in front of Mrs. Halliday's ice cream shop, and I pulled my bike out of the back. LeVon nodded toward the shop, which Mrs. Halliday had expanded to include dry goods. "People find a way to make ends meet."

That was true enough, and I wanted my family to do it without Victor's help, or anyone else's. We could take care of ourselves. We had to.

I walked into the sheriff's office. He leaned back and—I think—rolled his eyes. "Miss Mateo. Come to check again on your friend's case? Or are you digging out tidbits for Barry Hansen?"

I pulled out the moonshine jar. "This was on Ginny's property. The ranch hands say it belonged to Roy."

"Of course they do. I've already had five people—five!—come by to report a suspected communist, and three are sure they're living next door to a moonshiner. I should send the bill for the extra hours to Barry."

"But this has to do with the murder. Isn't there a way to find out who the bottle belonged to?"

He sighed. "Yeah. Comparing fingerprints is as hot as jazz these days. I took Roy's fingerprints when we brought in the body and Ginny's when we questioned her. I'll have to take yours if you touched the jar."

"I did. And so did Sam Ellis. Maybe some other ranch hands."

"I'll get to them later. I have some communists to investigate first."

The sheriff dipped my fingers in ink and pressed them onto a paper, rolling each finger side to side. When he was done, I tried to wipe my fingers off with the handkerchief, but the ink had sunk between the faint raised lines on each finger, and I couldn't remove the stain. I hoped I was doing the right thing by interfering again.

CHAPTER THIRTEEN

Sunday started with the usual tension. This morning, Mother had fresh, warm cinnamon rolls as her weapon of choice, while Abuela armed herself with her own version of migas made with eggs, leftover cornbread, and sizzling bacon.

Before the showdown could begin, though, someone knocked on the kitchen door.

Mother and Abuela paused their work in confusion. Papa walked past them to answer the door.

"Morning, sir." Victor looked in and gave Mother a charming smile. "Morning, ma'am."

He wore a white shirt and a tie, his shoes polished and his blond hair combed to a shine with Brilliantine. He looked good. Hollywood-star good, especially with that flashing grin and the twinkle of mischief in his eyes. He caught me staring and winked. I rolled my eyes and turned away to hide my blush.

"Oh, are you coming to church with us, Mr.—uh, Brother—Holbrook?" Mother asked.

"If I may, ma'am. I haven't had the opportunity for a while."

Abuela looked a little disappointed at his alliance with Mother, though vindication sparkled in her eyes when Victor had double helpings of her migas. Otherwise, the presence of a guest brought an armistice to the hostilities, and I even dared to have an extra cinnamon roll.

"Time to get the car," Papa said when breakfast ended. "*Vámonos*."

Javi bounded outside. I followed slowly enough that Javi could sit next to Victor in the back, and I was left to squeeze in next to my brother. The car bounced along the dusty road, joining with others coming into town for morning services.

When we parked and Javi climbed out, Victor leaned in to me.

"Okay, Sherlock. Now, we find some clues."

The normal buzz of chatter in the meeting hall had a sharper edge than usual, and it picked up more when Victor walked in. He brought his "flying circus" with him wherever he went. He strutted around the crowd, greeting giggling women with that brilliant smile. Sytha Chamberlain was quick to attach herself to his side. I simmered a little at her batting eyelashes and coy smiles. I was *not* jealous. I just hated to see people feed Victor's ego. And I was certain that Sherlock and Watson never found clues that way.

Sister Taylor sidled up to Mother. "Do *you* know who it is?"

Mother and I exchanged a glance. "Who what is? Is this about Ginny Hamblin?"

"What? Oh, no. The bootlegger!"

"Bootlegger?" I asked.

"Yes. Everyone's talking about it. Someone in town is a bootlegger. We have to find out who! I wonder if it's one of those Paiutes. I heard that Mrs. Halliday had to kick one of them out for trying to buy all the cough medicine and drink it."

"She had to do the same with old Mr. Walker," Mother said coolly. I was sure she had not forgotten that Sister Taylor's maiden name was Walker.

Sister Taylor stiffened a little. "Nevertheless. Oh, there's Sister Young. Maybe *she* knows something interesting."

Mother sighed when we were alone. "This is going to be trouble."

"The bootlegger rumors? You mean for the Indians?"

"For everyone. I just hope it doesn't turn into a witch hunt."

"Will people take it that seriously?"

"If they have nothing better to think about."

"You mean, like a murder?"

"They may connect the two in their minds, whatever the facts are. If they don't just forget the first matter entirely."

Like dogs distracted by a fresh, meaty bone. I bit my bottom lip. Was that better or worse for Ginny?

I spotted Sam lingering on the edge of the room. He watched the gossiping congregation with disgust. Ginny stood off to the side, arms folded, her expression stiff. Bits of the rumors were still about her. And about anarchists in our midst. Everyone gossiped a little at church—it was a small town and neighbors knew each other's business—but this seemed much more virulent than usual, spreading faster than influenza.

We made it through a service focused on the dangers of worldly influences like alcohol and un-American politics, and Ginny slipped out quickly when it was over.

Victor watched her go, his expression hard to read. Then, he wandered over to talk to Sytha Chamberlain.

"I'm going home with Ginny," I told Mother and hurried to catch up with my friend.

She was walking to her Model T by herself, Sam having left during the sermon. When I met up with her, she nodded a greeting, and gratitude flashed in her eyes. How terrible it would be to feel alone in the midst of a whirlwind of gossip.

"How have things been?" I asked.

"All right, I suppose." She smiled ruefully. "I wish there was a market for jackrabbits, because I sure have plenty of *those* on my property."

"I stopped by your place and talked to Sam."

"Huh. He didn't mention it."

Odd. Was he hiding something from Ginny?

"I wanted to check…" I took a deep breath. Talking about feelings made me think of the war posters: *Loose Lips Sink Ships*. We weren't supposed to complain or show weakness. Morale had to stay high. But the war was over, and this had nothing to do with the locations of troops or submarines. "I wanted to check on how *you're* doing."

"Oh." She shrugged heavily. "I'm... I'm angry. I know I'm not like those other ladies at church, but people really believe I could've killed Roy?" She glared at the road. "How can I go back after this?"

"I don't know." I really didn't.

"Why do you keep going? Your family, I mean." She didn't meet my eyes. "You're not always treated kindly either."

I studied the dirt road and the fine red dust that clung to my shoes. In some ways, it would be easy to stop going to church, especially when it seemed like we were outsiders, anyway. We could pray with Abuela and Rosie, attend Mass when we had the chance. "I suppose my parents keep going because... because they feel like it's the right thing to do."

"Even when no one wants them there?"

"I asked Papa once. He said that even if the people don't want us there, God does."

Ginny frowned. "I wish that made it easy."

"I know. My Papa... sometimes, it seems like it's easy for him. Once he decides something is right, he just does it. I don't know if it's stubbornness or faith, but he doesn't let anything shake him. For my mother"—I smiled—"it's definitely stubbornness. Tell her she can't do something, and she will."

"But what about you?" Ginny asked.

"There are times I wonder. I guess I'm stubborn, too. The revolutionaries chased us out of Mexico. Because we were Mormons. Americans. Well, sort of." I shook my head. "But now, this is my home. I don't want to let anyone chase me away again." I didn't want to be a coward.

Ginny nodded. "Thank you. That's good to think about."

It felt good to talk about it, too, instead of smiling and pretending everything was fine. If only the soldiers returning from the Western Front were allowed to do the same with the burdens they had brought back. But society required them to suffer in silence, wearing masks of stoicism or bravado while their wounds festered beneath.

Ginny dropped me off at the homestead. I walked up the lane, the sun pounding down on me. Victor was waiting, leaning against a fence post and staring at the cows.

"Hi, Doll. I missed you after church."

"Oh? I thought Sytha Chamberlain was keeping you company."

He grinned. "Jealous?"

"No. But you make a lousy Watson."

"That's what you think!" He fell into step beside me. "What did *you* find out at church?"

"That people talk too much."

"I thought you wanted them to talk."

I shrugged. "What great discovery did you make?"

He frowned and stared toward the field where his plane waited for Monday's customers. "Bootlegging is a whole heap of trouble."

"You didn't know that already?"

"Guess I hadn't given it much thought."

"Do you think it has something to do with the murders? They could be about gold. Or communism."

"Gold? Maybe. But I don't see communism or anarchy being big issues here. You don't have any factories or mines. No mobs of workers to organize, no big bosses to agitate against. Different places, different problems." He gestured around us. "What are your problems here?"

"Not enough water. Homesteads going under. And, people are afraid of outsiders. Afraid of losing what we've worked so hard for to someone who comes waltzing in with all the advantages we don't have. To someone who hasn't earned it."

"People might kill when they feel threatened. Would anyone feel that way about Roy or the prospector?"

I thought about how people treated Casimiro or Ramón. Disdainful at times, but not afraid. "No, they didn't seem threatening. Most people around here wouldn't trust them, though."

We had reached the house. Victor stopped and regarded me solemnly.

"Do you trust me?" he asked, uncertainty in his eyes.

I turned to study him, not sure how to answer. "What is it you want?"

"I'm not sure. I'm looking for... something. Redemption, maybe? A reason for everything I've been through. Everything I've done. I guess I'll know it when I see it."

"Not gold? Or moonshine?"

He smiled humorlessly. "I don't think either of those will scratch my itch."

He opened the door for me, his expression troubled. I stepped into the kitchen, its warm, familiar smells comforting me. Neither Roy nor Vern had threatened the things that mattered to me: my family, our refuge on the homestead. But they obviously threatened somebody. Somebody who was desperate or hardened enough to kill.

CHAPTER FOURTEEN

The next morning, as I hung freshly wrung laundry to dry in the sapping heat, Sam walked up the road to our house.

"Morning, Brother Ellis," I called to him. "Are you here to see Papa?"

He shook his head and looked over his shoulder. "I just wanted to come over to apologize."

"Apologize?"

"I thought you were just being nosy like a lot of other folks in town. But you helped Miss Hamblin yesterday. You've been a good friend. This has been hard on her, and there's not much I can say." His eyes filled with pain. "I'm afraid I only make things worse if I try to be close to her." His dark cheeks flushed. "I mean, to show her support."

"Ohhh," I said, understanding dawning.

He smiled ruefully. "Don't worry. I'm no fool. Miss Hamblin is my boss, I'm an Indian, and…" He shrugged one shoulder. "Well, you know, she doesn't show much interest in fellows, anyway. She just wants her homestead and her freedom."

"I'm… I'm sorry."

"No need." He waved away my words. "Things won't change, and that suits me just fine. I'm an Indian orphan raised by white folks. I was never destined for the normal course of things."

"Maybe none of us were," I said softly.

He tipped his hat and walked away. He wouldn't want pity, but I could at least feel sympathy for him. It was hard to be in between. Did that make him feel threatened? I knew he would go the extra mile for Ginny, and now I knew why. A man in love could be dangerous.

I helped Mother and Rosie make a quick lunch for Papa and Javi to grab when they took a break from the fields. As we sliced and buttered bread, a pounding on the front door made us jump. Mother dried her hands on her apron and went to the door. Rosie and I watched from the kitchen entryway.

The pounding came again as Mother reached for the doorknob. She scowled and yanked the door open. The town marshal, Clyde Little, stood there, fist raised to repeat his knock.

"Yes?" Mother said crisply.

"Mrs. Mateo, may I come in?" the marshal asked.

Mother moved to block the doorway. "That depends. What brings you here?"

Marshal Little smirked. "Do you have something to hide?"

"Only a messy kitchen." She cocked an eyebrow. "Can I help you with something?"

"You can let me have a look around. I got word that I might find bootlegged liquor on your property."

Mother stiffened. "Who would say such a thing?"

"Anonymous tip." He was still smirking.

I slipped out the kitchen door before I could hear Mother rain abuse on him and the anonymous tipster. I needed to find Papa.

"Miss Mateo?" Victor stood from the melon patch, jogging to catch up with me. His trousers were dusted with red dirt from the garden. "What's wrong?"

I shook my head, too angry to explain, but not annoyed as I would have expected when he followed me to where Papa was working in the corn. Instead, there was something reassuring about having him silent by my side.

"*Mija?*" Papa caught my eyes. "What's happened?"

"Marshal Little is here. He claims we have moonshine."

Victor scoffed. "You don't, so you've got nothing to worry about."

"Not necessarily," Papa said. "Sometimes, all people need is an excuse."

He met my eyes, and we shared a look of understanding born in the Mexican Revolution. How you looked or spoke, what church you attended, even who visited your house, like Sam Ellis: they could all be sufficient pretext to be badgered and bullied, sometimes right out of your home.

"Well, I'm not going to let them—" Victor glanced back, and his eyes hardened. "Hey! Get away from that, you bumbling idiot!"

Marshal Little was standing on one of the biplane's wings, hanging on one of the cables while trying to peek into the cockpit. He jumped back but struck a defiant pose.

Victor stormed over, and I followed. "You think I'm hiding moonshine in my plane? With passengers in and out of it every day?"

"I just have to check—"

"You just want a free peek. You can pay like everyone else."

The marshal reddened. I cut a warning glance at Victor. His protectiveness over the Jenny was not going to help us with Marshal Little.

The marshal walked up to Papa. "You got any liquor on your property?" He spoke too slowly and clearly, like Papa didn't understand English.

"No, sir," Papa said.

"You're friends with some of those Spanish sheepherders, aren't you? I've heard they're not very respectful of the law. Might even be Red spies."

"Of all the—" Victor started forward.

I put a hand on his arm and pulled him back. "Please, don't," I whispered. "He'll find a way to get back at us if we cause trouble."

Victor tensed, but he didn't say anything else.

"I don't know any communists," Papa said.

"But you used to make wine, isn't that right?" Marshal Little asked.

"Well, yes. For the Catholic churches."

"And you still have the equipment here?"

"There's not much market to sell it right now."

"Yeah, I've heard your homestead is struggling. Might make it tempting to bring in a little extra money."

"I'm no bootlegger." Papa's voice was dangerously low.

"We'll see."

When Marshal Little was out of earshot, Victor whispered, "This is wrong. Your family wouldn't be involved in anything like bootlegging. You're good people."

"Sometimes it doesn't matter," I said quietly.

The marshal tramped around the farm, poking in the hay stacked in the barn and knocking over a couple of Mason jars in the root cellar. Mother watched, fists clenched and face bright red. My stomach knotted, and I had to look away or I saw the soldiers in the revolution raiding our home again. Violating our space and our peace.

"When I find out who..." Mother muttered.

Papa shook his head. "Retaliating won't do us any good."

Mother's eyes glittered, and I suspected her revenge would be subtle and savage.

But who would do this? Mother had offended Sister Taylor at church. Bo Young would take any chance he could get to cause trouble for us and try to drive us away. Or did someone know I was snooping around, and they wanted to teach us a lesson?

I couldn't watch any longer. I hurried for the Model T and cranked it up. Barry Hansen might have more letters for me, though they were starting to cause more trouble than they were worth.

By the time I reached Kanab, my heartbeat had returned to a slower pace. The town went about its business as usual, its rhythm set by the turns of the seasons and cycles of the weeks. I was finally able to buy Rosie's radio wire, then I stopped by the print shop.

"What brings you here?" Barry asked, motioning me into the cramped-but-organized space.

"Off the record?"

He laughed. "Of course."

"Someone suspects Papa is a bootlegger. They're turning the homestead inside out."

"That's silly," Barry said. "You need water for making moonshine, and you guys haven't got a lick to spare."

"That's true enough. Who do *you* think is making moonshine?"

"Oh, I'm sure a few people are. I doubt we have any real bootleggers around, though. There's not much of a local market, and someone would notice it moving in and out of town. It's hard enough getting legitimate crops to market."

"Yes, it is!"

Which was interesting. If Roy and Vern's deaths were related to bootlegging, the killer had to be someone with water to spare and a way to deliver the liquor undetected.

Bo Young, perhaps? Even he couldn't have much excess water with the extra cattle he was running. But his son had been drunk. Mel was afraid his father would find out—because Bo Young didn't approve of drinking, or because he didn't want his son dipping into his profits? Roy and Vern might have found out, or they could have been moving the liquor for him and tried to double cross him. That would be a dangerous secret.

"Oh, good news for our friend Ginny Hamblin," Barry said. "The sheriff said the bullets couldn't have come from her gun. She's in the clear."

"That's wonderful news. Thank you!"

Ginny was justified, at least in the eyes of the law. The rumors would follow her until the real killer was found, though. It was still hard to think one of our neighbors could have done such a thing. Maybe it was an outsider sneaking liquor through Kane County to sell it on the reservations, willing to kill anyone who caught him. Someone Roy and Vern knew? If so, someone needed to stop him, but discovering the culprit would be especially dangerous. With my friend in the clear, though, I could leave that task to the sheriff. Roy and Vern weren't my ghosts.

CHAPTER FIFTEEN

Victor continued in his usual devil-may-care way, showing off his plane and bowing for the crowds. I watched everyone who came to the homestead with sharper eyes. Brother Brown laughed too hard at someone's joke. Was he nervous? Tipsy? How did all these struggling farmers have extra cash for airplane rides?

I rubbed my aching forehead and returned inside. These were my neighbors. They worked the land the same as we did, attended the same church, shopped at the same little stores. I had to leave the investigating to the sheriff.

When the crowds left, Victor joined Mother, Rosie, and me in the kitchen where we chopped potatoes and breaded chicken. He pulled a wad of bills out of his pocket and plunked them in the change jar on the counter.

"Your share of today's take."

"Thank you," Mother said as she measured flour to thicken the gravy. "It will make a big difference to us."

"Glad to be able to help, ma'am." Victor grinned at me.

I turned back to the potatoes, not sure what to think of him. He paid us as promised. He understood the war. But he had lied about when he came to Kane County, and he had that mysterious connection to Roy Shelton.

Mother paused in stirring the gravy to stare at the lengthening shadows outside. "Javi should have been back from the Briggs' place hours ago."

"He's probably flirting with some girl," Rosie said, not looking up from dipping strips of chicken in egg and bread crumbs.

A worried line still creased Mother's forehead.

"I'll take the Model T and pick him up," I said.

Victor stood. "I'll go, too. It's a nice evening for a ride."

Mother raised an eyebrow, but at the moment, I didn't care if she had the wrong idea. With all the gossip about bootleggers and communists—with a killer still lurking around town—I didn't mind having company.

I took off my apron and hurried outside. Dark clouds hung low overhead, and the air smelled like rain.

"Can I drive the Tin Lizzy?" Victor asked, gesturing to the Model T.

I gave him a warning look.

"No?" He smiled that Hollywood-worthy smile and pretended to cock a gun. "I'm shotgun, then."

"Just get in the car."

I started the engine, and we drove up the road toward Pahreah.

"Why are you so anxious to come along?" I asked.

"Why are you so anxious I don't? I thought we were friends."

I didn't know what we were. "I don't want you putting ideas in Javi's head. He's already restless."

"Then those ideas are already in his head." Victor stretched his arm out across the back of the seat. "You can't keep him tied to your apron strings."

"My 'apron strings' have been soaked in blood in the trenches. He doesn't know—doesn't understand."

"And you want to protect him. I get that. But you're going to have to let him do *something*. If you're always pushing him down, he's going to shoot off in a direction you don't expect or like. Let him play guitar in a Dixieland band, make a few home runs on a travelling baseball team, go to college in a couple of years. Trust him a little. He won't be a kid much longer." Victor grew quiet, then added, "And if people are going to do stupid things anyway, maybe the best thing we can do is make it as safe as possible for them."

I glanced over at him. He sounded uncertain, like he was trying to convince himself more than me.

Victor studied the darkening sky. "Any ideas where we should look for him?"

"He was supposed to help the Briggs work on their fences today, so we'll start over there."

But Brother Briggs scratched his head and frowned when I asked about Javi. "He left a couple of hours ago. Maybe he stopped by the Chamberlain place?"

"I'll check, thank you."

"Is it usual for your brother to wander off?" Victor asked as we hurried back to the car.

"No."

I grabbed the metal crank of the Model T. Javi was restless, but he wasn't irresponsible. Hurt, though? Possibly. He might have encountered a mountain lion or a rattlesnake. Even a coyote could be dangerous if Javi was injured.

We drove off toward the Chamberlain's ranch, the wheels rumbling over the washboard road as I pushed for more speed. My teeth felt like they would rattle out of my jaw, but it was getting dark, and at any moment the sky might open in a downpour and unleash flash floods.

"Look!" Victor grabbed my arm and pointed.

Two figures stumbled across the sagebrush-studded desert.

"Javi?" I stopped the car and hopped out.

One of the figures saw us and veered in our direction.

"Javi!" I raced forward, rabbitbrush snagging at my skirt.

Was he drunk? No, he was supporting his companion. Casimiro. The Spanish shepherd dragged one leg. His eye was swollen shut, and blood crusted his cheek.

I stumbled to a stop in front of them, Victor right behind me. "What happened?"

Javi moved as if to shield me from Casimiro's injuries. "Ten, you probably shouldn't—"

Victor put a hand on Javi's shoulder. "She was a nurse. She's seen much worse than this."

Javi looked back and forth between Casimiro and me as if seeing what the war was for the first time.

Victor and Javi helped Casimiro to the front seat of the Model T, and I examined his injuries. "Your ankle's not broken, but your nose is. I'll need to set it. And we should clean the cuts on your face so they don't get infected."

"I shouldn't be away from the sheep for long," Casimiro said weakly. "There are coyotes."

"We'll tell the Chamberlains so one of them can watch them—just for the night," I said. "You won't do the sheep any good in this condition. Now, tell me who did this to you."

Casimiro pressed his lips together. I glanced at Javi, but he shrugged. "I didn't see it happen; just found him after."

I stared down Casimiro. "I smell alcohol on your breath. Did you start a fight with someone?"

"No!" he looked terrified at the suggestion. "I swear. I did drink a little. It is very dull just watching the sheep. It was not so much that I couldn't think right, though. I would never do that." He looked down. "But Marshal Little and some of his friends caught me. They called me an anarchist and a bootlegger. Said I should go back where I came from. But I can't go back to Asturias. I never made my fortune." He turned an imploring gaze on each of us. "You see, you cannot tell anyone what happened. I am not an anarchist, but I was drinking."

"That doesn't mean you deserve any of this," I said. "Javi, tell the Chamberlains that Casimiro had an accident. He'll be back tomorrow, but he needs medical care tonight."

Javi nodded and dashed off.

"I'll go with him," Victor said. "Safety in numbers when there are bullies about."

"Thank you. I'm taking Casimiro home."

Victor jogged after Javi, and I got the car running.

"This is too kind of you," Casimiro said as I drove him back to the homestead.

"Nonsense. Mother's making dinner, and we'll need help eating the leftovers."

Casimiro laughed weakly. I didn't suspect him of anything worse than sneaking a drink, but with this kind of attention from the marshal, it might not be long before the sheriff took notice of him. And I didn't think of Casimiro as an outsider, but most of our neighbors would.

"You're not making your own moonshine, are you?" I asked.

He winced and shifted in the seat. "No."

"Where do you get it?" I felt like I was interrogating a prisoner, since Casimiro couldn't escape my car, but I needed to know.

"It's… it's the kind of secret a lot of people know about. There's a sandstone cave where you can put a bit of money, and when you go back, someone has left the moonshine."

"How long has that been going on?"

He shrugged a little. "At least since last year, probably longer."

That made sense. Our corner of the country had been going dry in pieces, first Utah, then Arizona, New Mexico, and Nevada, before the nationwide ban. Someone with a small moonshining business could have expanded it over the past few years into something quite profitable.

Someone local.

"Where did you hear about this cave?" I asked.

He sighed. "I don't remember. It's like a rumor. Many of the young men whisper about it."

So, maybe that was where Mel got his alcohol, too. But who was the moonshiner?

I helped Casimiro into the house. Mother's cheeks turned an angry red when I whispered to her what happened. She and Abuela hardly waited for me to clean Casimiro's injuries before they started fussing over him.

Javi and Victor arrived home later, and the scene took on the tone of a party, with Papa and Javi playing music to entertain our invalid guest, and Mother, Abuela, and Rosie keeping him well furnished with food.

I watched quietly from the side, and so did Victor. I couldn't guess what he was thinking, but he looked troubled. I turned away and opened a window, and the sharp scent of wet sage warned me that the storm had arrived.

CHAPTER SIXTEEN

Crowds continued to gawk at Victor's biplane and pay for rides in the days leading up to his airshow on Saturday. I hoped Mel would come by so I could prod for information about the moonshine, but the Youngs stayed away at this point.

Since Sister Harris from Pahreah had seen Victor at church, she decided she could trust his piloting skills, and now she took her turn in the biplane. The bystanders craned their necks to watch it dip and soar against the background of the red cliffs.

A man tapped me on the shoulder and sheepishly asked, "Has your grandma got any more of those 'cro-ket' things? Boy, those were good."

"We're all out today," I said, trying not to smile at his obvious disappointment. Abuela was practically dancing the Charleston in the kitchen over how popular her cooking had become.

Victor's plane banked and descended toward the red dirt airstrip its wheels had carved into our green pasture. As it drew closer, the plane shuddered in the air. Smoke billowed from the engine, which sputtered and coughed.

The crowd gasped and rushed forward. A few people ran onto the airstrip, into the path of the plane.

"Move!" I hurried through them, pushing them out of the way. "Give him room!"

The people skittered aside like startled sheep, but they kept their eyes fixed on the plane, which dropped fast toward the airstrip, black smoke trailing. I was close enough to see Victor wrestling the controls. Sister Harris gripped the edges of her cockpit. I crossed myself and prayed.

The wheels hit the ground hard. The plane bounced back into the air and swerved to one side.

The crowd shouted.

The plane came down again, skidding and hopping violently. It rolled along for a time on one wheel. The people surrounding me gasped. The tip of one wing skirted the ground, and for a moment I was sure the plane would tumble over, but the machine jerked upright again and bounced onto both tires. The wooden rear landing strut snapped off and cartwheeled across the field. The biplane jolted along, kicking up a trail of dust.

At last it settled to a stop. The engine emitted a few final mechanical hiccups before sputtering out.

The crowd went silent. A cloud of dust and engine smoke passed over us, gritty in my nose and mouth. Then Victor climbed onto the wing, took a bow, and helped his trembling passenger out, motioning for the crowd to clap for her. She smiled weakly.

"Sister Harris got her money's worth," one man proclaimed, and everyone laughed and cheered.

Sister Harris clung to Victor as he helped her off the wing, her face ashen. She tittered nervously once her feet were on the ground.

"No more rides today, folks," Victor called. "But don't miss the big show on Saturday!"

The crowd slowly dispersed. I pushed through them to reach Victor. His jaw was tight as he examined the engine.

"You're all right!" I said.

"As you see." His words were light, but his eyes blazed darkly.

"Is your plane damaged?"

He finished his inspection and said curtly, "Nothing too serious. I think the fuel was running too lean and overheated the engine."

"That was excellent flying. You saved Sister Harris's life."

He shrugged.

"Accidents happen," I said. "You don't blame yourself?"

"What, for that landing? Of course not," he growled. "That was an amazing landing. I deserve a medal for it."

Did he want *more* credit? I folded my arms. "Well, everyone was impressed."

He whirled on me. "Impressed? Is that what they are?"

"Yes?"

"Wrong!" He backed me up against the wing. "What they are is bloodthirsty. It's not enough that man can fly. It's not enough that this hunk of wood and cables can glide up there in the clouds like men have been dreaming of since Adam. No. They want more excitement. They want to see smoke and danger and maybe a little blood on the field."

"No! I'm sure they would have been horrified."

"You think so? Wait until the airshow, *sister,* and you'll see that I'm right." He gripped one of the cables next to my head. "You heard about Arch Hoxsey? Died setting a new altitude record in California? Do you know what the audience did when his plane smashed into the ground?"

I shook my head weakly.

"They rushed the field. Not to try to save him. Oh, no. They wanted souvenirs. They stole parts of the plane splattered with his blood."

I looked away. Victor didn't let me off that easy.

"And Lincoln Beachey—he was the greatest aviator the world will ever see. Buzzed over the White House in his plane to convince President Wilson that we needed the Air Service. Tried to help military pilots by teaching them his maneuvers. But it was the death-defying tricks the crowd and the press screamed for. People died trying to copy his tricks, but the audiences pushed for more and more." Victor's face was close to mine, his words hot. "His plane crashed in the ocean trying to answer their thrill-lust. The impact didn't kill him. His fingers were bloody from trying to claw his way free as he drowned. The crowds killed him!" Victor smacked the side of his plane and turned away. "What do they care about blood, as long as they're entertained? As long as they get to say they were there when it happened. Roman coliseums or nice little Mormon towns; they're all the same."

I'd heard the jump rope song about Beachey.

> *Lincoln Beachey thought it was a dream*
> *To go up to heaven in a flying machine.*
> *The machine broke down, and down he fell.*
> *Instead of going to heaven he went to . . .*

My stomach twisted.

"Why do you do it?" I whispered.

"What else am I supposed to do? They needed boys to go over there and fight and probably never come back. Those fellows in Washington, they love blood just as much as the crowds." He ran his hands through his hair. "But I did come back, and I brought all my ghosts with me. Nobody wants us to talk about the war. It's in the past. *Eat, drink, and be merry*, they say. *Forget it*. Well, I can't forget it!"

He gave me a desperate, pleading look.

I took his hands gently. "Neither can I. The field hospitals were bad, and the trenches when I saw them. But in one village..." I took a shaky breath. I had never spoken of this. The words came slowly. "They'd dug tunnels. When the zeppelins or the planes came over, we had to go down. Into the dark. And once when the artillery hit..." I squeezed his hands, but nothing else in Utah seemed real. France was all around me again. "Everyone was dying. Bleeding. Suffocating in mud. It was so black. Just screaming and crying. I couldn't help anyone."

My eyes burned, but the tears wouldn't come.

"I'm sorry." His tense fingers relaxed against mine. "We're the ghost talkers—you and I. The voices of the dead. We know the truth, and we have the scars to prove it wasn't so glorious." His grip tightened. "But no one wants our stories or our scars. Put a bandage or a tin mask over it." He squeezed his eyes shut and pulled his hands away. "They just want to be merry. Well, fine. I'll give them merry."

He jammed his hands in his pockets and strode off.

CHAPTER SEVENTEEN

Victor ate with us that evening, but he didn't say much as Javi blathered on about the heroic landing. When Victor smiled to thank Mother for the dinner, it didn't reach his eyes. Lincoln Beachey and the bloodthirsty crowds had snuffed out his humor. At the airshow on Saturday, though, Kane County would prove to him that not everyone was the same.

"Come listen to the radio," Rosie invited him as Mother and I cleared the table.

Victor hesitated, then shrugged. "Sure, why not."

Papa and Javi's music drifted into the kitchen as we cleaned up, and I scrubbed the dishes quickly so I could join them. Victor stood apart from the others, studying my petrified wood collection through the glass. I walked over to him.

"You've got some interesting pieces in here," he said quietly.

"I've been collecting them since we moved here seven years ago." It probably sounded childish.

"May I?" Victor gestured to the handle of the curio.

I nodded, and he opened the glass door and lifted a large chunk of petrified wood, its rings preserved in bands of red and orange.

He ran his fingers over the rings. "I feel like I'm holding a piece of the past."

"That's why I like it. It's beautiful, and now it will last forever."

He gave me an understanding glance. "That's comforting, isn't it?"

My face warmed, and I nodded.

He turned the piece over a few more times, his expression too serious to be thinking only of petrified wood. He traced the rings again. "It can't die or change, but it also can't grow."

He put the piece of wood back and gently latched the door closed.

I stared at my collection. My reflection in the glass door frowned, looking troubled.

A knock at the door interrupted Papa and Javi's music.

Mother answered and stepped back to let the visitor in. "Sister Young?"

Bo Young's wife pushed past Mother and beelined for Victor. Her eyes were red-rimmed. "Please, I need your help!"

Victor put a hand on the woman's arm. "Steady there. What's wrong?"

"Mel went riding this morning. His horse came back without him. We've been looking, but he could be anywhere. And I hoped, with your plane…"

I glanced at Victor, remembering his harsh words earlier that day. But his face softened, and he looked at the fading light streaming through the window. "Of course, I'll fly out and see if I spot anything."

"Thank you!" Sister Young said. Then, she lowered her voice. "Please, don't tell Bo I came here. He wouldn't like it."

Mother nodded and looked at Victor. "It'll be dark soon."

"I flew night missions, ma'am. If there's a moon tonight, I can search for as long as I have fuel."

"I'm coming, too," I said. "If he's hurt, you'll need a nurse."

Mother looked unhappy, but Victor nodded. He asked Sister Young a few questions, and then we dashed out for the newly repaired plane.

Victor tossed me the flight cap and warmed up the engine. I climbed into the front cockpit and fidgeted in my seat, unable to get comfortable. The orange globe of the sun sank into the horizon, but the pale half moon hung above us like a lantern. Mel could have fallen into a ravine or encountered a mountain lion. I clutched the flight cap. And then, there was a killer on the loose.

"We won't be able to see much once we lose the light," Victor called as he climbed in behind me. "You look right, I'll look left."

I nodded and fastened on the goggles, the rims biting into my face. We taxied down the pasture and jumped into the air. I remembered the plane's hard landing that afternoon but put it out of my mind and focused on scanning the ground.

Victor flew north to the jagged canyons and cliffs. The sunset touched the poplars on the homesteads behind us with gold, but the shadows stretching over the ground muddied everything below into shades of gloom. Victor buzzed low, and the ever-present jackrabbits darted away. Nothing else moved. The dark lumps could be sagebrush or boulders or bodies. Bodies strewn over a battlefield.

No. Not here.

The chilly wind numbed my face, but I leaned out. A ravine dropped beneath us, a dark gash in the landscape, and Victor nosed down to follow it. My stomach lurched, and I had to force myself to keep my eyes open. Keep looking. Mel could be down there. If he was injured, every minute mattered. A man could bleed out in minutes. Or go into shock. The desert got cold enough at night for hypothermia, especially if his clothes were wet. Morning and daylight would be too late.

And if a killer had found Mel...

I shook my head and squinted, trying to make sense of the shadows.

The planed veered, and I looked to the left. Victor pointed to a human-like silhouette huddled on the edge of the mesa. I shook my head, not sure it was anything more than a scrubby bush, but the figure moved, turning to watch us.

"Where can we land?" I called over the rumble of the engine.

"I see a flat spot," Victor yelled back.

I saw nothing that looked flat, especially not in the uncertain light. I gripped the edges of the cockpit as we dropped. The wheels hit with a jar that rocked me to the side, slamming my elbow against the cockpit. The plane bucked and pitched. I shut my eyes and prayed as we bounced over the ground, tearing through sagebrush and slowly coming to a stop.

"Are you all right?" Victor called.

"Yes." I tore off the flight cap and scrambled out of the cockpit, my legs still shaking.

Victor hopped down beside me, and after a brief inspection of the Jenny, he scanned the mesa where we'd landed. It was fairly flat and dotted with sagebrush and juniper, which made it harder to spot the figure we'd seen from above.

"There," I said, pointing to where something dark shifted against the pale orange of the sunset.

We jogged across the hard ground to where the mesa dropped off into the desert below.

Mel sat on the edge of the cliff, tears running under his tin mask to drip onto the rifle sitting in his lap. He tensed when we approached.

"What are you doing here?" he snapped, laying a hand on the stock of the gun.

"Your mother was worried about you." Victor crept closer to him. "She wants you home."

"No one wants me at home." He tightened his grip on the rifle, glaring at it. "I'm such a coward. I couldn't do it. I can't live like this, but I don't want to die."

"Of course, you don't," Victor said, edging nearer.

"I'm scared of the dark now," Mel whispered. "Everything is just so dark."

"I know," I whispered, not meaning to speak, but not able to stay silent.

Victor lowered himself to the ground next to Mel, his eyes on the rifle barrel. "Hey, there's going to be light again."

"I can't see it," Mel said, his voice cracking.

"I know. I know," Victor said. "But it's just on the other side of the horizon."

"All I see are nightmares. Even when I'm awake. Even when I

drink. The nightmares are always there." He lifted the rifle, running a finger over the cold curve of the trigger guard. "I just want them to stop."

Victor laid a hand on the gun. "I get it, friend. You can't outfly them either, I've found."

"What's the use of me, then?" Mel jerked the gun up.

The barrel swung near Victor's face, but he didn't flinch. He kept his voice steady.

"Hey, life is sacred, right? Even if you're not who you want to be right now, you've still got that spark of the divine in you."

Mel wiped his dripping tears with his sleeve. "Right. Look at me."

"I am looking at you," Victor said. "Now I want you to look at me. Come on, look me in the eyes so I know you're hearing what I say."

Mel's gaze stayed fixed on the sight at the end of the rifle. He twitched it back and forth, a silvered pendulum ticking off the silent moments as the light died.

The swinging slowed.

His hands stilled, and he met Victor's eyes.

Victor leaned forward and put a hand on Mel's shoulder. "You are not this moment, right here. You are not the war. You are not a tin mask. You are not shell shock. You hear me? Those are things that happened to you—and they shouldn't have—but they are not *you*."

Mel stared blankly ahead, but his grip on the rifle slackened. Victor slid it away and handed it to me. I held it tight.

Victor helped Mel off the edge.

"I'm sorry," Mel said. "I shouldn't have caused so much trouble."

"Don't say that," I said quietly. "We're glad you're back."

Mel nodded and limped mechanically along the edge of the mesa.

I looked at Victor, who watched Mel go.

"I don't know," Victor said.

"What?"

He met my gaze. "You're wondering if I really believe all that stuff I just said. I don't know. There are times I've thought about how easy it would be to just nose over too much, and me and Jenny would be gone like that. But then I remember those war-mongering politicians who were willing to throw lives away—my life away—like so much ash from a cigar. Some days I keep going just to spite them."

"Yes," I said, more fiercely than I meant to. "Don't ever... don't ever quit. Please."

"You mean that?" he asked softly.

I nodded, hoping the approaching darkness hid the red in my cheeks. "I'm not always sure about things, either. But you're right about that spark in everyone. I saw it go out too many times, and every time, the world got a little darker."

And that was why Roy mattered, and Vern, too. I hadn't known them, but someone had snuffed out their sparks, and that hurt every one of us. It seemed, standing there on the mesa, that Victor felt it, too. That I wasn't so alone with my burden.

Victor glanced at the fading glow on the western horizon. "Speaking of dark..."

"Yes." I sighed inwardly. The moment was over. We were several miles from anywhere, and the plane would only hold two. It seemed unwise to leave Mel to walk back on his own, and I didn't want to trek to the homestead alone in the dark, killer or no killer. "You can ferry us back one at a time, or I can walk with Mel."

"I don't want to chance that landing again. I'll fly back and borrow your parents' Tin Lizzy to come meet you, if you can get down from the mesa."

"We'll manage." At least we would be home before dawn if he drove, and with the moon up, it wasn't completely dark. "You can find this mesa again?"

"Sure. Once I've seen a place from above, I get a pretty good map of it in my head. One good thing that came out of the war."

I nodded and handed Victor the rifle. "He doesn't need this right now."

Victor took it. Not long after, the Jenny circled over the mesa and headed back toward the homestead. Mel and I picked our way down from the mesa in thoughtful silence. I couldn't ask Mel anything about moonshine at that moment, but I'd had a good look at the rifle. It was a 3030.

CHAPTER EIGHTEEN

When Saturday came, I woke before the sun. Muffled voices spoke outside my window. I sat up and pulled my blanket around me, ready to call for Papa.

The airshow.

I groaned and laid back down. The flying circus would be in full force today with crowds tramping around the homestead and scaring the cows.

And then it would be over.

We'd have our cut of the tickets. The neighbors would leave our homestead in peace. Victor would be gone.

I peeked outside. Lines of cars and wagons crept up the road and across the pasture. A few people had even set up tents. Had they spent the night? At least they were respecting the fence protecting the crops. We'd prove it to Victor: Kane County wasn't perfect, but it was a safe haven.

Mother had breakfast ready, and Abuela wore the dress she usually saved for trips to Mass.

Javi ran in from the yard. "You won't believe the crowd! People are coming from everywhere—even Cedar City and St. George!"

"We'd better eat if we want to be able to see," Papa said.

"Can we sit on the roof?" Javi snatched a slice of bacon from the table.

Papa shook his head. "If we do it, everyone else will, too, and I don't know how much weight it can hold."

We scarfed down our eggs and bacon and hurried outside. The spectators overflowed from the planted pasture, kicking up a gauzy cloud of red. Barry had printed programs, and local boys hawked them along with popcorn. The air smelled like butter, salt, and dust, and voices buzzed around us, punctuated by laughter. In the distance, the plane engine warmed up.

"Any of those Spanish dough things?" one of the men asked Mother.

She smiled and shook her head. Today would be too busy. Papa and Mother headed off in different directions to help manage the crowd. Abuela grabbed Javi, Rosie, and me and, with the ferocious determination of a Spanish grandmother, somehow forced the crowd to part for us until we found a seat on a split-rail fence with a good view of the red ruts carved into the green pasture by the plane's wheels.

I waved to Ginny, who had ventured out for this event and sat nearby using *Vogue* magazine for a fan.

Victor prepped the plane, checking the cables and struts. The girls sitting near us giggled.

"He's handsome!" one girl said.

"Let's hope he doesn't crash and break his pretty face," grumbled the young man next to her.

"I wish he'd take me flying." The other girl rested her chin on her hand and sighed.

Javi chuckled quietly and nudged me with his elbow. I rolled my eyes. Still, I did feel a bit of pride when I thought that I had flown with Victor. That I actually knew the man behind the smiling bravado that wowed the crowd. Silly.

At nine sharp, he taxied down the runway. People leaned forward to watch him lift into the air. Some gasped and clapped just at that. Victor banked over the house to come around and do several loop-the-loops directly overhead. Several audience members screamed and ducked. He followed that up with barrel rolls and spins, and the audience cheered themselves hoarse.

Abuela's posture was tense, and she shook her head at his stunts. I clenched my fists when he did a sharp dive, pulling up at the last minute and spraying a cloud of dust over the audience. They roared in appreciation.

"*Madre mia!* Unnatural," Abuela muttered.

But the crowds loved it, cheering for more daring, more risk.

"I've heard of pilots who walk on the wings," one of the girls in front of us said. "I want to see him try that!"

In another low swoop, Victor tipped his wing so it looked like he was going to hit the ground. The audience leaned forward like a single, hungry animal. At the last moment, Victor pulled up into another loop-the-loop. Several people groaned at the save. My stomach tightened.

The plane pulled up into the blue. Higher. Higher. What had Victor said about the altitude record? That pilot had died. When the plane was almost too far up to see, it came barreling toward the ground, tumbling head over tail like a playing card thrown into the air.

People jumped to their feet.

"He's going to crash," someone screeched.

Excited.

I gripped Javi's arm. His face had gone pale, his eyes wide in horror. Rosie gaped. Abuela crossed herself and mumbled a prayer.

The head-over-tail fall turned into a corkscrew spiral. Controlled. I let out my breath. When the plane was almost to the ground, Victor jerked the plane sideways in another spiral.

His head connected with the windshield.

Several spectators around me whistled and cheered. I stood, my hands to my mouth. Had Victor been knocked out?

He turned the plane in a wide circle over the audience. No, he was still flying. The audience settled down. Some of them looked bored now.

I pushed my way out of the crowd, ignoring the dirty looks of my neighbors as they strained to see past me to the next near-miss. Or bloody crash. That would entertain them, too.

Victor was right. Barry Hansen. Betty Lou. Sister Brown, the Relief Society president. The Briggs and the Chamberlains. All my mild neighbors, with their worries about hairstyles and cattle prices, roared for blood. They didn't know. When they'd had a taste of real blood, they would choke on it. It would give them nightmares and wait for them in the dark, tight spaces away from the sunlight.

"Get away from that fence!" I snapped at some young men who had scrambled into the rows of squash for a better view.

They scurried away under my glare. I turned back to watch Victor bump down into a safe landing.

He jumped from his plane and bowed. The crowd hooted and waved their arms. Victor was smiling, but not really. It was a toothy grimace, and his eyes were full of disgust that echoed my own. I suddenly felt I had nothing in common with these people cheering around me. Could they belong to the same species as the dying boys who had cried for their mothers as artillery shells rained down on us? Who laughed too loud or drank or stared into some inner world to try to escape the smell of blood, the metallic tang of it in their mouths that made every meal taste bitter?

I guarded the crops with a stony stare as people congratulated Victor or snuck closer to gawk at the biplane. Slowly, the crowds thinned out, and some of the angry tightness in my chest relaxed.

I turned to stare at the cliffs. Keeping the world out? No, fencing me into my own little corner, not better or safer than any of the rest of it. There was nowhere to hide from the sickness I had seen on the battlefield.

Someone took my arm. Victor. He had removed his flight cap, and a red welt showed on his forehead.

"It was like I said?" he asked.

I nodded, my eyes full of tears.

Victor's hard expression softened, and he brushed my cheek gently. "I'm sorry."

I grabbed his hand and held it there, desperate for the warm touch. The knowledge that I wasn't so alone.

"Victor Holbrook?" asked a voice behind us.

He lowered his hand and turned reluctantly to face the sheriff. "Yes?"

"You need to come with me."

Victor gave the sheriff an incredulous look, then smiled sourly. "Everything in my show is perfectly legal."

"But maybe not everything you've been carrying in your plane." The sheriff hitched his thumbs through his belt, his right hand close to his pistol. "We found your fingerprints on a jar of moonshine belonging to Roy Shelton, and more on bottles at a local cave known as a hub for the distribution of illegal liquor."

"No!" I said. "He wouldn't."

Victor *had* known Roy. And he had lied about coming to Kanab. But he had also helped Mel. He knew moonshine was dangerous. He wasn't a criminal.

Then again, I hadn't believed that my neighbors would cheer for blood. Maybe everyone wore tin masks to hide coyote eyes and rattlesnake smiles.

Victor clenched his fists. He wouldn't look at me.

"We'll be investigating you for bootlegging," the sheriff said, "and for the murder of Roy Shelton."

CHAPTER NINETEEN

Victor's shoulders slumped. "All right, sheriff, I'll go with you."

That wasn't right. He was supposed to protest the injustice. Tell us he was innocent. But he just walked away. I didn't want to watch, but I couldn't make myself move as Victor climbed into the sheriff's car. They drove off, and the dust settled behind them.

Then, I wanted to run. To hide somewhere and sort out the jumble of questions in my head. But this was my haven, and it didn't feel safe anymore.

The breeze tumbled an empty popcorn bag against my leg. I grabbed it and crumpled it.

Javi ran up to me. "Where's Victor going with the sheriff?"

I glanced up at my family and Ginny, all watching with concern. "They think he might know something about the bootlegging. The sheriff's asking him some questions."

Victor couldn't be a killer. There had to be a good reason for his fingerprints on the moonshine. No need to worry anyone. Javi frowned, but my family returned to cleaning up. Ginny stayed, watching me from the shadow of her straw bonnet. I stooped to pick up discarded programs and cigarette butts.

"And?" Ginny asked.

"And what?"

She grabbed a paper cup and held it out for the cigarette butts. "None of this is just about bootlegging."

"No." I tossed in the ground-out stubs. "It's about murder."

"They think your pilot friend might have done it?"

I nodded.

"And you don't?"

I glanced at the plane. "I don't... I don't think so."

"Well, you knew I wasn't a killer, so I believe you about him, too. What are you going to do?"

"What can I do?" I stomped along the fence line, snagging up another discarded program bragging of daredevil stunts. "When the sheriff mentioned the moonshine, Victor looked... defeated. He lied about Roy and about when—and probably why—he came to Kanab. His fingerprints were on the bottles. He lied about everything."

"Bootlegging doesn't equal murder."

"Moonshine kills people." I pictured Mel. "It hurts people."

"True." Ginny squinted across the way toward the barn. "Does Mr. Holbrook have a gun?"

I crammed the rest of the trash into the paper cup. "I don't think so." He hadn't been armed when we found Mel stumbling around the yard.

"Can't shoot someone without a gun."

"That's true."

"You don't *want* to help him?"

"I don't know. I thought... I thought I understood him. That we understood each other. But he's been tricking me this whole time. Maybe using me."

I should have kept my pain to myself. Not leaned on anyone else.

Ginny studied me, her lips pursed. "Possibly. But if he isn't the murderer, then the guilty person is still out there."

I frowned at my collection of trash. Whatever Victor's guilt—however he might have betrayed my trust—I didn't want to see him falsely accused. "The sheriff will sort it out."

Ginny snorted. "Sure, he will. It's really convenient to blame things on an outsider. He might just let a jury sort it out. Besides, whatever questions the sheriff asks him, it won't satisfy the questions *you* have."

I gritted my teeth. I didn't want her to be right. "I suppose I could take Mr. Holbrook some of his things at the jail, assuming he's not back by tonight."

Ginny nodded and returned to helping me clean.

Victor didn't return by dinner. The family was very quiet, and when I announced I was going to take Victor his packer trunk, no one made any objection. I retrieved it from the barn, tempted to open it and see if he did have a gun. I ran my hand over the leather punctuated with brass nails. No, the sheriff would handle this.

I drove to Kanab as the sun dipped toward the western horizon.

"Miss Mateo," the sheriff said when I knocked on his door. "Looking for a scoop for Barry Hansen? Or on another mission of mercy?"

"The latter." I hefted the trunk. "Since Mr. Holbrook didn't return, we wanted to make sure he had his things."

The sheriff took the trunk into his office and rummaged through it. I tilted my head to peek, but he found nothing suspicious among the shirts and trousers. "I'll bring it to him."

"I'd like to talk to him, if I may."

Sheriff Moore hesitated.

I stepped up to rest my hands on his desk. "The town marshal has already checked my father's homestead once looking for moonshine. I'm sure Mr. Holbrook's arrest will bring us more unfounded accusations. I want to clear everything up." I raised an eyebrow. "You can even listen at the door."

The sheriff rolled his eyes, but he smiled a little. "All right. I'm not leaving you in a closed room with him, though. I don't want to give him any chances to make trouble."

"Fine by me."

He showed me to the same room where he'd questioned Ginny and, a few minutes later, brought Victor downstairs. Sheriff Moore motioned for him to sit and went out into the hall, the door standing open.

Victor folded his hands on the table, not meeting my eyes.

"Moonshine?" I whispered.

He smiled humorlessly. "No need to keep quiet about it. I confessed the bootlegging to the sheriff already."

I winced. It was true, then. "Why?"

Victor rested his forehead in his hands and rubbed his temples. "I needed a way to survive. Most of the big airshows want you to do even more dangerous stunts, and I wasn't interested in that."

"There are other jobs."

"Not that let me fly." He met my eyes. "And I figured that people are going to drink, anyway. Better to drink some safe, smuggled alcohol than something nasty they made in their bathtub." He looked out the window. "If it makes you feel any better, after seeing the effects of the stuff, I regret it. And I definitely want to see the killer locked up. Especially instead of me." He smiled a little then turned serious again. "I'm sorry."

"For bootlegging?" I asked. My lips felt numb. All of me felt numb.

"For not telling you the truth. I liked spending time with you. I didn't want you to know what I was."

I opened my mouth then shut it again. I liked spending time with him, too. I did not like that he was a bootlegger. That he had deceived me.

"I did try to clue you in to what I knew," Victor said. He lowered his voice. "That's why I sent the letter about the moonshiner."

"The Miss Grace letter?" I whispered, glancing toward the hall where the sheriff waited. So, Victor *had* been paying attention to the papers in the desk.

He nodded and winked, holding a silencing finger up to his lips. "You asked about Roy Shelton before? I met him a couple of times. He was my contact. Showed me where to pick up the moonshine that needed to be flown out of town. But I didn't shoot him, and I don't know any prospectors." He leaned so that he was talking to the sheriff as much as myself. "And Roy couldn't have been the one behind the moonshining. Whoever contacted me did it through telegraph signal, and Roy didn't have anything to transmit or receive one. He was just a middle man."

I remembered Rosie's translated messages. *Meet me tonight.* But she had no way to track who was sending the signals. "You do think Roy's death is connected to the moonshining, then."

"Yep, and I'll tell you something else. There's some money in moonshine, but not enough to kill over. At least, not in southern Utah. I think the moonshiner is hiding something else as well."

I sat back, taking that in. But it was probably meant more for the sheriff than for me.

"Thanks for bringing my clothes," Victor said.

I nodded.

"Are you taking care of the Jenny?"

"It's right where you left it."

A smile crooked the corner of his mouth. "Good to know. Keep her safe for me."

"Time's up, Miss Mateo," the sheriff said.

I nodded to Victor and the sheriff and walked out into the gathering gloom. I believed him, in spite of everything, but that left me with the feeling that the killer was breathing down my neck, and I wouldn't rest easy until the real danger was behind bars.

CHAPTER TWENTY

The sound of the airplane engine clicking to life woke me Sunday morning. The house was still. Mother and Abuela had not yet risen for their weekly battle in the kitchen. I grabbed my robe and rushed outside, ready to confront a kid trying to steal a joy-ride. The predawn chill and the scent of dew on alfalfa hit me as I hurried to the field.

Victor stood in the dim light. I pulled my robe tighter and walked up to him.

"You're out!" I called over the engine.

He glanced at me then at the light warming the top of the cliffs. "I am."

"Did they let you go," I asked cautiously, "or did you have to post bail?"

"Neither. I broke through my ceiling into the attic and squeezed out window then hiked from Kanab."

I wondered if I was supposed to laugh, but he wasn't smiling. "You're serious."

"Yep. The sheriff arrested me for bootlegging. They're not going to let me post bail until they can bring me in front of a judge, but I imagine they'll be really quick to pin everything on me, and all while the killer walks free." He shook his head. "I'm going to prove my innocence."

Now I did want to laugh, but more out of shock than humor. "By breaking out of jail and flying away?"

"I'm not going far, and I'll turn myself back in when I'm done. You can tell the sheriff that when he comes looking for me." He smiled a little. "I imagine he'll realize I'm gone soon, and he'll have an earful to say." His expression turned serious, and his gaze lingered on my face. "I didn't want you to think badly of me, though."

I didn't know where to look. "I think... I think this is a crazy."

He laughed. "It probably is, but here's what I figure: Whoever was selling that moonshine is being awful secretive about it, even for Prohibition. I think they're making the stuff out in the hills some-where where they don't want to get caught. Maybe they're doing something else illegal, too. But if I find them, I can prove that I had nothing to do with the murders."

"You've seen the desert from the plane, but I don't think that gives a fair idea of how vast and empty parts of it are."

"Sure, but no one can trek out there and make moonshine without leaving a trace. They would need water. A trail to move the liquor to the cave. And I know where the cave is, so I can start from there. I make maps in my head when I fly, remember?"

It was a long shot, at best, but we had managed to find Mel when he was missing. And Victor had already burned his bridges with the sheriff. "Good luck, then."

I stepped back as Victor taxied down the pasture and took off. Mother and Abuela watched from the kitchen doorway. I joined them there.

"What happened?" Mother asked.

"He broke out of jail to prove he's innocent."

"*Virgen Maria!*" Abuela crossed herself.

Mother shook her head. "Well, we'd better eat before the sheriff gets here. I'm not sure we're going to make it to church today."

Abuela looked gleeful at that.

As we ate breakfast and cleaned the dishes, I alternated between watching for the sheriff and listening for the return of the plane.

The knock came first.

Papa opened the door to Sheriff Moore.

"Can I help you?" Papa asked.

"I need to ask about Victor Holbrook. He around?"

"He's not a killer," Mother said, coming up behind Papa.

The sheriff puffed out his cheeks in an exasperated sigh. "When was the last time you saw him?"

"The plane took off this morning," I said quickly, before Mother made it sound like we were aiding and abetting a fugitive. "I don't know exactly where he went, but I believe he'll be back."

The sheriff took off his hat and scratched his head. "Normally, I'd say you're being naïve, but here's the thing. Some of the kids this side of Kanab are telling a story, and I'm not sure what to make of it." He looked like he wanted to come in and sit, but Papa still blocked the doorway. "They said they saw his plane flying low around the hills this morning, and then there was a pop, and smoke came up from the engine. They said it wasn't like when he landed with Sister Harris. The plane dropped pretty quick. I was hoping Holbrook made his way back here, because if not, I've got a search on my hands."

I covered my mouth.

Mother's face paled. "Did the children see where the plane went down? He might have landed it safely, like he did here in the yard."

"They just said back in the hills to the north. It was moving too fast for them to see exactly."

Papa grabbed his hat. "I'll help with the search."

"Me too!" Javi stood beside Papa.

"I'm going to tell Sister Brown," Mother said. "The Relief Society will want to do something to help."

I wasn't so sure. Victor was an outsider and an admitted bootlegger. They might say he brought it on himself.

But the town surprised me again.

Everyone in Pahreah turned out to search for Victor, and people came from Kanab and Fredonia, not to gawk or gossip, but ready to help. The same people who had clamored for disaster in the air show now left church and crops to scour the hillside on horseback and by foot.

"I don't understand," I told Ginny as we hiked over a sandstone ridge, searching for the plane. "There was such a vicious side to them, but now they're..."

"Generous?"

"I suppose, yes."

She sighed. "I think we're all of us at least two people inside, part animal and part, well—"

"Divine?" I asked, using Victor's word. "There's too much of the animal."

"But enough of the divine, if we look for it."

I had seen both sides of Victor. The one who justified bootlegging liquor and the one who saved Mel. And both sides of myself too, if I was being honest.

I only returned home when there was no more light for searching. I entered the living room to find Mel Young sitting with Rosie, both huddled over her radio.

"Keep trying," Mel said.

Rosie scrunched up her forehead in concentration and moved the antenna wire just a fraction.

Javi looked up at me. "Mel had a great idea to use the radio."

"Use the radio?" I looked between them.

"He had a telegraph on his plane," Mel said without looking up from Rosie's work. "So, he could send messages to the ground."

I drew a sharp breath. Of course. I huddled closer and chewed my thumbnail as Rosie worked her magic with the crystal and wires.

The radio clicked and crackled through the headphones.

"Stop!" Mel said.

We all jumped, except Rosie, whose hands froze in place.

"That's it!" Mel looked to Rosie, who nodded.

"Morse code?" I asked.

Mel turned in a circle, his gaze darting frantically. "Give me a minute." He found a pencil and paper and started scribbling. "There!"

He held up the message.

nw hamblin ranch shot down danger

CHAPTER TWENTY-ONE

I leaned over Mel's shoulder to read the message again then looked at Rosie. "Is there more?"

"No, it just repeats." Her face was pale, and she held the wire very still, our thin connection to Victor, wherever he was. If only we could message him back. Speak to him.

"NW Hamblin Ranch," Javi said. "So, northwest of the Hamblin Ranch?"

"Sounds that way," Papa said. "I'll go let the sheriff know. As soon as it's light, we'll focus the search out there."

Papa put on his Stetson and headed out.

The rest of us stared at the radio. The pattern of crackling coming through the headphones ended abruptly. Rosie tensed and moved the wire in tiny increments, looking for the signal.

Mel shook his head. "It stopped."

"Maybe he's resting," Javi said. "He must be tired."

"Yes, he's just resting." I stared out the window at the darkness.

"He said 'shot down danger,'" Mel said quietly.

"He might not be thinking clearly," Mother said.

"Could be." Mel didn't sound convinced.

Abuela crossed herself and prayed to Saint Anthony, the patron saint of lost things.

We slowly broke away from the radio, except Rosie, who sat next to it with head bowed, as if expecting an answer to prayer to come through in Morse code.

I stood by Mother. "I'm going to Ginny's place. I want to be closer when the search starts."

Mother nodded. "Sister Hamblin will want to help, too."

I packed a clean blouse and overalls and wheeled out my bike. I pedaled hard, trying to outrun the ghosts lying in the darkness under juniper bushes or in dry washes, echoes of faint voices calling for my help. The moonlight reflecting off the dirt road guided me through the nightmare and up the winding road to Ginny's house. The yellow lamplight from her living room beckoned me back into the present.

I left my bike leaning against the porch and knocked on her front door.

She peeked out her window then hurried to let me in.

"Tenny! Is there news?"

I nodded and told her what happened.

She gestured down the hall. "Help yourself to the guest room. It sounds like we'll want an early start."

"You think the sheriff will use your place as a base?"

She snorted. "If he has the guts to ask, he'll be welcome. But *we'll* want to get out there first thing, won't we?"

"Victor's message did say 'danger.'"

"Then he needs help."

I nodded. We would head out at dawn.

Ginny woke me as soon as the eastern sky began to turn gray. We grabbed a quick breakfast and headed out to find the other searchers gathered on the road in front of Ginny's homestead. Sheriff Moore gave us a look of barely contained exasperation.

"We've got it all covered, ladies. There aren't many places north-west of here. It's mostly just mesas."

"Plenty of little gullies and ridges in those mesas," Ginny said. "It'll take a lot of people to search all of them."

Sheriff Moore shook his head. "I've got my search party here. I don't want to have to worry about anyone else going missing."

Papa, who was standing in the group with Javi and Mel, gave me a knowing look and a slight nod. I nodded back and put a hand on Ginny's arm before she mounted a verbal offensive against the sheriff.

Sheriff gave his final orders to the searchers, and they scattered to begin the hunt. Ginny turned and stormed back up to her homestead.

"That man!" Ginny said.

I caught up with her. "We're going anyway. Papa knows. But where should we search that the others won't already think of?"

Ginny turned and studied the lay of her ranch, the breeze fanning through her blonde bob. "What exactly did the message say?"

"NW Hamblin Ranch shot down danger."

Ginny squinted as the sun broke over the cliffs. "The sheriff's right about one thing. There's not much directly northwest of here but mesa. It's got a lot of scrubby trees. A crashing plane would leave an obvious trail there. But the northwest corner of my ranch is hilly. Lots of places for a pilot to go missing. Lots of places for a shooter to hide, too, if there is one."

And Victor knew Ginny's homestead pretty well, having flown over it many times. "Let's go!"

Ginny called for Ramón to saddle a couple of horses and instructed Sam to lead the other ranch hands in checking the rangeland again for any signs of plane or pilot.

"Tenny and I are headed up to the cliffs," Ginny finished.

Sam looked concerned, but he nodded. "Stay safe, boss."

Ginny grabbed her 3030 rifle from the house, and Ramón brought the horses around for us. I carried only a canteen, some bandages, and my Beacon flashlight. While the long morning shadows still stretched down from the cliffs, we rode west. The ground quickly turned rough, thick with sagebrush, spiny yucca, and scraggly junipers. Jackrabbits darted away from us, and Ginny took a potshot at a coyote skulking in the distance.

She led us into a dry wash. On either side, knobby red sandstone pillars carved by wind and water towered over us like the crumbling ruins of an ancient temple. The sandy wash made slow going for the horses. The sun rose higher, and the shadows of the cliffs seemed to shrink away from us. Sweat trickled down my back, and my mount swatted flies with her tail, her steps faltering to a plodding pace. Victor wouldn't survive long in this heat.

"We can't go much farther on horseback," Ginny said. "Even the cattle don't usually make it this far. Not that they have much reason to, now that it's gone dry."

I nodded. The sandstone pillars had given way to stone walls and steep cliffs pocked by caves worn out of the sandstone. The wash narrowed to a slot canyon ahead.

We dismounted and left the horses. Ginny led the way as we squeezed through the narrow slot and scrambled up the rocks. The canyon walls provided respite from the heat but narrowed our view to the red rocks surrounding us. As I pulled myself up to a rough sandstone ledge, the sun glinted off something ahead.

"What's that?" I pointed. "Is it part of a plane?"

Ginny squinted. "Only way to find out is to climb over there."

We scrambled down to face a staircase of boulders going back up that probably formed a waterfall when storms came. Now, cracks fractured the ground into parched squares, their edges curling like leaves scorched by the sun. We picked our way up the ascending ledges of the ravine. I paused to wipe sweat from my face and sip carefully from my canteen. Ginny's land was dry, dry, dry. There was no way to replenish if we ran out, and the desert sun would show no mercy to a lost man caught under its glare.

Finally, we came to the top, and the wash leveled out again. I had been looking for broken bits of glass or metal, but I gasped. Victor's plane lay in the wash, one battered wing dangling lopsided.

I scrambled down to it. "Mr. Holbrook! Victor!"

Ginny jogged right behind me. "Is he..."

I peeked into the cockpit. "He's not here." I touched the radio. The leather flight cap lay discarded on the seat. No signs of blood there or anywhere around the plane. No signs of danger. "But he was here last night." I surveyed the scene. The wash led to another ravine carved out of the steep sandstone. "Maybe he moved to those cliffs to get more shade." I glanced back at Ginny. "I'm going to look for him. He's probably banged up. You bring the sheriff or some of the searchers in case we need to carry him out."

Ginny nodded and climbed back over the edge of the dry waterfall. I searched the cockpit further. No useful supplies. The telegraph might still work, but I didn't know Morse code or if Rosie would even be listening.

Water had once shaped the dirt in the wash into soft, flowing rivulets, but it was an illusion. The sun had baked it into a hard crust. No footprints broke the smooth pattern—not from Ginny or I, and not from Victor.

"Victor!" I called again.

My voice echoed off the ravine walls, and then the deep silence of the desert fell again. A raven flapped overhead, the beating of its wings loud in the stillness. The only danger I saw was the heat and the lack of water, which would both be worse for an injured man. Victor might have been delirious when he sent his message, and that was the night before.

I clutched my canteen and hurried toward the cliffs. A little sagebrush clung to cracks on the side of the ravine, but otherwise the wash was barren, carved out of the sandstone at some past time when flash floods had roared down from above. A fist-sized rock in the scattered gravel caught my eye. Petrified wood. A good omen. I stuck it in my pocket and jogged along the ravine walls, searching for signs of life.

I glanced up and saw a promising shelter under the rocks overhead. If I were Victor, that's where I would go. I slung the canteen strap over my shoulder and climbed, glad I had on overalls instead of a dress. The path wasn't as hard as I expected, with natural ledges in the cliff leading me to the shelter.

It was more than just an overhang. The shelter pushed back, deep into the heart of the cliffs. Into the thick black, like the tunnels during the Great War. I stared into the darkness, my heartbeat loud in my ears.

Another sound reached me. The burble of flowing water echoed from somewhere within the cave. But where did it come out? I strained my eyes against the dimness. Fresh drag marks scraped across the floor and out of sight.

"Victor?"

The darkness threw a mocking echo of my weak voice back at me then swallowed it. Erased it.

Victor might have injured his leg, pulled himself toward the promise of water. I had to go after him. But the blackness rose in front of me like a wall. Gaunt faces with glassy eyes stared at me from the dark, their pale hands outstretched in unheeded supplication. My stomach heaved, and I scooted back into the warmth of the sun.

A darker spot on the sandstone floor caught my eye. And another. Leading into the darkness. Blood. None by the plane, but a trail of it here. Danger.

My fingers brushed the blood. Dry, but recent enough not to be covered with dust. Whoever had left the trail—Victor?—had lost a lot of blood. Was probably still losing blood. He would die before more help arrived, if he wasn't dead already. Beyond my help. Another failure. Another light snuffed out. No more laughter, no more surprising insights, no more warm understanding.

But if he was still alive...

The ghosts whispered out of the cool stillness of the cave. Screams of terror. Screams for help. All my running from my nightmares, and here they were, waiting for me. My mouth was too dry to swallow, and tremors rolled down my arms. My limbs locked in place. I could not move.

I had been wearing a tin mask like everyone else, but now the darkness peeled it away, and I saw myself reflected there. I wasn't a bloodthirsty predator beneath my mask. I was the cowering prey. Hiding from soldiers in Mexico. Hiding from artillery shells in the tunnels. Hiding from the world on the homestead.

"I can't help," I whispered to the ghosts in the darkness. "I'm sorry. You know I can't."

But what about Victor? I wiped my palms on the rough denim of my overalls. My fingers brushed the lump where the petrified wood sat in my pocket. Lovely, safe, but unchanging. Dead.

I was the only help here. I could be as stubborn as Papa—as Mother—and I was tired of being chased away by nightmares. I was tired of hiding. I had to try.

CHAPTER TWENTY-TWO

The darkness waited. My mind filled the void with France and the dead men I had not been able to help, but I had to push past them. I crawled forward a few feet and stopped. I had reached the edge of the light, and my eyes adjusted enough to see a bit further, but then the blackness turned complete.

I fumbled for my flashlight. It would give away my position, but I would never find anything in the cave without it. I clicked it on, and its pale yellow circle spread out over the sandstone floor. I crawled forward, taking the little bubble of light with me.

Ahead, something reflected the light onto the ceiling and walls in shimmering waves. I held the flashlight higher. The water. It seeped in from the back of the cave and formed a deep, clear pool. Once, it may have filled the cave floor and flowed down the terraces I had climbed to reach it, but someone had built a dam to hold it back. Only a trickle escaped on the far side, gurgling toward an unseen exit.

A dark shape loomed beside the dam. I crawled closer, casting glances at the darkness pressing in on all sides. The mass resolved itself into a wooden tub and a box of bottles. It was a still. I had found the bootlegger's lair.

But who built it? The bootlegger was someone who knew every

pocket and fold of Kane County. Ramón, perhaps, or Casimiro? The ranch hand or the shepherd might know about such a remote place, but I didn't want to imagine them as killers. And whoever ran this still had probably shot Vern when he came across it. Roy, too—maybe when he objected to Vern's death. The bootlegger also had access to a telegraph to send messages to Victor.

Speaking of which. I stood and scanned the cave with my flashlight. There, that lump of ground by the wall that could almost be just rocks and shadows.

"Victor?" I whispered.

Nothing. I crept closer. The curled-up form was Victor, but he wasn't moving. I sank next to him on the ground, my fingers icy. Was I too late? Failed again? But his skin was warm, and he drew shallow breaths. I said a silent prayer of gratitude while I examined him. He looked unharmed except a bloody goose egg on the top of his head. As if he had been struck.

"Victor?" I shook him gently.

He groaned and opened his eyes, flinching at the light. I shone the flashlight away, but even in the dimness, his pupils looked too large, one wider than the other.

"What happened?" I asked, trying to get him to focus on me.

"I guess I fell asleep." His speech slurred. "It's cold. Where am I?"

I braced him with one hand. "You're in a cave. In Kane County. Do you remember how you got here?"

"Oh, heya, Doll." He smiled weakly. "Say, it's pretty cold. Where am I?"

Confusion. Not a good sign. Did he actually recognize me, or did he just happen to call me Doll? My chest tightened, but I forced a smile back. "You're in a cave, but it's time to go. Come with me. No! Don't stand yet. Let's crawl."

"Yeah, I don't feel so hot. Where are we?"

We scooted along the sandstone floor, Victor unsteady on his hands and knees.

Something tickled my hand. I glanced down to see a tarantula crawling up my arm.

I froze, goose bumps prickling over my skin. I wanted to scream and flip the giant spider away, but that might agitate Victor. It wasn't poisonous. Just terrifying.

A light flashed over me. I gasped and put out my spider-free hand to steady Victor.

"Miss Mateo?" called a voice from the cave entrance. "Is that you?"

LeVon Banks stooped there, shining his flashlight in. I released Victor to shield my eyes. He turned his head from the light.

"Mr. Banks! I was afraid it would be hours before help could get out here." I called, trying to shake the tarantula loose. It raised its front legs at me, and I went still.

"I wasn't too far away. Is that your pilot friend?"

"He's injured. I'll need help getting him down. Is anyone else coming?"

"More help will be right behind me." LeVon kept his flashlight in my eyes as he walked forward, but he focused his gaze on the still. "Well, well. What do you make of this?"

I looked between him and the tarantula. "Uh, someone dammed up a spring to make moonshine, from the looks of it. Ginny will be glad to have the water back once she hears."

"Won't she, though?" LeVon asked with a dry chuckle. More of a cackle.

Victor squinted at the mail carrier, confusion and suspicion warring on his face.

I turned my full attention to LeVon. He had gotten to the cave very quickly. Too quickly. Ginny could not have found him so soon. But, as a mail carrier, he knew everybody and everything in Kane County. He knew the land well enough to notice where there might be water. He had a telegraph. He was always scheming to make more money.

LeVon turned back to us.

"You go first," he said. "I'll take care of Victor."

I smiled and brought my free hand over to the tarantula. I grabbed the huge spider and hurled it into LeVon's face.

LeVon screamed and swatted at the creature.

I grabbed Victor's arm and pulled him forward.

He groaned and crawled after me toward the light, wincing at the brightness. "I think I'm going to be sick."

"Keep moving."

LeVon shouted and swore behind us, his flashlight waving madly until he dropped it. He flung the tarantula away and grabbed a rifle.

I pushed Victor to the edge of the shelter. "Go! Zig-zag your way down. Try to kick up some dust."

Victor started his unsteady climb, and I turned back to LeVon. He raised his rifle. His 3030. I leapt forward and shoved it aside, sending his first shot into the ceiling. The gun's kick knocked him off balance, and bits of sandstone showered down on us. I grabbed the rifle barrel, still hot from the first shot, and slammed my boot into LeVon's knee.

He collapsed and rolled to the front of the cave, scrambling down the incline after Victor. I scurried behind him.

Victor half-crawled, half-slid down the path. LeVon skittered along like a lizard. I fired the gun, striking next to LeVon and sending shards of sandstone flying. Hopefully, that let the searchers know we were in trouble.

LeVon looked back and snarled. I fumbled for the chunk of petrified wood and threw it, connecting with his forehead. He swore and rose to face me.

Victor reached the bottom.

I charged down, jumping from ledge to ledge to catch up. LeVon flinched from the avalanche of sand and pebbles hailing down on him and turned again for Victor. I swung the rifle like a club and hit LeVon's shoulder, sending him tumbling down.

When LeVon landed in the sand at the bottom, Victor rolled on top of him, pinning him down by weight instead of skill. I leveled the gun at LeVon's head.

"You wouldn't!" LeVon spat. His friendly mask was gone, and his lips curled back to show his gold tooth.

A predator's snarl. There was no place I could hide from the world's problems, but that didn't mean I had to keep running from them.

I cocked the lever. "You can't leave a coyote loose in the flock."

LeVon went still. Victor stayed put, though his face was ghostly pale. I kept the rifle locked on LeVon as the sun inched its way across the sky. Sweat trickled down my back. I wondered which of us would succumb first to the heat. Probably Victor.

"Tenny!"

I didn't glance up at Ginny's voice, but the rush of blood in my ears eased. Sheriff Moore ran forward and hauled LeVon off the ground. Victor curled up, cradling his head and looking meek as a lamb in the sheriff's presence.

I lowered the gun and swallowed hard to keep myself from vomiting. My hands trembled, and I was only too glad to let one of the deputies take the rifle.

"LeVon tried to shoot us with it," I said, proud and surprised that my voice sounded so matter-of-fact. "I'll bet the bullets match the ones that killed Roy and Vern."

The deputy nodded his thanks. I turned and gagged. Our postman had murdered two men. Had been willing to murder Victor and me. Over what? Booze. Money. And one more thing.

"Wait!" I said. "There's a still up in that cave." I looked at Ginny. "And a dammed-up spring. He was diverting your water."

Her eyes widened and then narrowed. "Bo Young knew," she whispered, too low for the sheriff to hear. "His cattle were always wandering onto my property."

I nodded. He was taking LeVon's advice about the cattle and maybe splitting the profits with him. He probably counted on the water from Ginny's property to help with his extra stock, and LeVon was likely helping him with his land grab. If Bo knew anything about the murders, I doubted LeVon would protect him. But I also thought LeVon played his cards close.

CHAPTER TWENTY-THREE

I stood among my rose bushes, armed with thick leather gloves and clippers at the ready. Musky perfume wafted from the soft, gently curving petals. I hated to clip a single flower, but I had to keep the bushes healthy. Bees hummed around me as I worked.

The hum grew louder, and the cattle in the fields scattered. A biplane buzzed overhead. I froze, images of war fleeting past me. Then I took a deep breath, and my hands relaxed.

"He finally got it flying!" Javi raced over to watch Victor land in the pasture.

I followed more slowly, a little sorry to see the plane in the air. I should have been happy that our homestead could return to normal, and that Victor had his freedom restored. The sheriff had let him go with a fine and "time served" for bootlegging, and now he would take to the skies again. LeVon was the one going on trial for murder.

Ginny had found the pool catching the diverted spring water. Plenty of cattle prints marked the ground, but there was nothing to prove that the stock belonged to Bo Young. LeVon claimed to know nothing about any of it. A jury would decide.

Victor wasn't alone in the plane. He helped Ginny out of the passenger seat. She'd finally had her chance at a free ride. After all, the plane had been stuck on her property while Victor replaced the parts ruined by LeVon's rifle shot and the crash.

Ginny carried something in her arms. It looked like a ball of living fluff.

"Is that a dog?" Javi asked.

She laughed. "It's a rabbit."

"Really?" Javi poked at the fur. "Wow! It's so soft!"

"It's angora." She smiled at me. "I figured if my property is so good for jackrabbits, maybe wool rabbits would thrive as well. I'll keep them in a dugout so they don't get too hot, and people pay a fortune for the wool. It's all the rage."

I held my hand out to the creature. It sniffed me, its breath warm on my skin, and then I stroked its silky wool. "I can see why!"

"I just have to shear them a few times a year to collect the wool. It's easy to transport, too," Ginny said. "Having that spring back will keep the crops alive, but these darlings are going to make the homestead secure."

I nodded. After everyone in town raved about Abuela's croquetas, Betty Lou had arranged with us to sell them in the diner. We all found ways to survive, like LeVon said.

I wanted to believe it was some inherent madness or moral deficit that led LeVon down the path to murder, but that need to get by—to do a little better and sleep securely at night knowing the happenstance of the next day wouldn't be enough to drive you under—made it hard to define the line that marked "enough." And once you cross one line, the next one is a bit easier.

I glanced up. Victor was watching me, his eyes curious and intense.

Ginny looked between us and smiled a little. She held up the rabbit. "Here, Javi, do you want to hold her? I'm trying to think of a good name. Maybe Victoria. Or Josephine? Something regal."

"Regal?" Javi laughed. "It's still a rabbit, no matter what people pay for the wool. You should call her Roast or Stew. No, Pie!"

She lured Javi out of earshot.

Victor traced the toe of his boot through the red dirt. "So, I need to keep moving."

"I know."

"Have you ever thought about a life in show business?" He grinned. "You'd look great as a wing walker, Doll."

I rolled my eyes. "No, thank you."

"Yeah, actually, I'm not keen on that idea either. I'm going to find a way to fly and make a living that doesn't lead me down the same path as Linc Beachey. I can't impress the ladies if I'm dead."

I raised an eyebrow. He brushed back a strand of my hair that had come loose from its pins, and his thumb traced a path down my jaw. I drew a surprised breath at the warmth that flushed over my skin. He leaned in and kissed me, his lips lingering for a moment. Then, he winked and strolled off after Ginny and Javi.

I glared after him. Presumptuous man! The next time he came to Kane County, I wouldn't be so tongue-tied, and I'd give him a piece of my mind. I touched my jaw, still warm where he had caressed it, and followed the others back into the house.

AUTHOR'S NOTES

I hope you enjoyed *Blood in a Dry Town*. Please remember to leave a review.

The "Mormon" Colonies in Mexico

Colonia Juárez was one of several "Mormon" (Church of Jesus Christ of Latter-day Saints) colonies in the Mexican state of Chihuahua, not far from the Texas border. Many Anglo Latter-day Saints fled there to escape persecution for polygamy in the United States in the 1870s, as well as to proselyte to their Mexican neighbors, a few of whom converted. The colony flourished until the Mexican Revolution of 1910 forced most of the (mainly Anglo) residents to flee back to the United States. Some settlers returned once the area settled down, and the colony and its school are still a unique cultural region today.

Hispanic Immigration to Utah

Though the 1920 census lists no Hispanics in Kane County (and the census taker was obviously confused about how to list the status of Anglo children born in the Mexican colonies but now living in Utah), World War I draft registration cards show that several men from northern Spain were living in Kane County, working as shepherds or laborers. Their lives went mostly unrecorded, but they were among the growing Hispanic population of Utah in the early 1900s, including migrants from New Mexico and other parts of the Southwest, immigrants from Spain, and refugees from the Mexican Revolution.

Immigrants struggled during this time as a rise in nationalism and fear of communism due to the Russian Revolution made many people hostile towards "outsiders." Several widely publicized cases made people believe that anarchists were hiding in every dark alley, and Italians and other Southern Europeans were especially suspect.

Kane County in 1920

Pahreah or Paria (rhymes with "Maria") is now a ghost town, and by 1920, it was almost completely abandoned. Despite this, the area was open to homesteaders in the 1910s, an era when homesteading boomed in Utah. I have given Pahreah a little longer lifespan than it actually enjoyed so the nefarious actions of schemers and murderers could be confined to a semi-fictional location and population.

Dr. Norris was the real doctor for Kanab and Kane County at the time, and Mrs. Halliday ran an ice cream shop and general store, but the other characters are fictional. The sheriff in 1920 was Sheriff Swapp, and Will Dobson and Jack Borlase produced the *Kane County News* around this time, eventually merging it with the *Garfield County News* in Panguitch, with Kanab's blacksmith, George M. Shields covering Kane County. I didn't want to implicate any of them in any behavior inconsistent with their real character, so I invented alternatives. Julius Dalley was the real postman in 1920, and I feel confident that he was innocent of LeVon Bank's crimes.

Kane County, and the rest of Utah, sank into an early "Great Depression" following World War I. Kane County residents were creative in trying to keep their farms and businesses afloat, including trying new types of livestock like buffalo. I don't know if angora rabbits were among the animals any of them tried, but the rabbits' remarkably soft, warm wool became popular in the US around this time. Though there is a lot of misinformation about angora wool online, it is usually harvested humanely by plucking it free when the rabbits naturally molt their coats or by shearing several times a year. Angoras are friendly because they have to be handled often to care for their wool, and many people who raise them regard them as pets instead of livestock.

Kane county did have its own notable illegal escapades during this time. A rancher was accused of poisoning a rival neighbor, though the jury acquitted him. A criminal escaped from the jail in Kanab by climbing out the attic window. The no-alcohol-and-tobacco policy that Latter-day Saints are now well-known for was not yet strictly enforced in this period, so bootlegging was rampant during Prohibition even in Utah. Moqui Cave, just north of Kanab, was rumored to be a speakeasy during the 1920s; it later became a bar and dance hall for the Hollywood stars who flooded Kane County and is now a museum.

Kane County remained very isolated and technologically delayed during much of the 1920s. Road improvements and electricity only came during the mid- to later part of the decade. While the more privileged class in New York City were drinking at speakeasies and dancing on rooftops under electric lights, in Kane County, people still used oil for heating and light. Amateur radio was banned during World War I, but it flourished again after, with new innovations making crystal radios nothing more than a hobby item within a few years as vacuum tube radios brought entertainment into American homes.

Barnstormers and Tin Masks: Lingering Effects of World War I

Following World War I, the US Army sold off some of its surplus supplies, including thousands of Curtiss JN-4 "Jenny" biplanes used for pilot training. With a flood of pilots experienced in tricky maneuvers meant to avoid enemy aircraft and a high unemployment rate, many former pilots began travelling from town to town to put on stunt shows, which soon became known as "barnstorming." As during the war, the death toll for these pilots was very high, but some, like

Lincoln Beachey, seemed unable to walk away from the challenge. The first airshow came to northern Utah in 1910, when simply taking off in Utah's high altitude provided severe challenges. Utah's position as the Crossroads of the West brought more pilots across the state after World War I, but it appears to have been well after the period of this book before airplanes were a common sight over southern Utah. Most people in Kane County would not have seen an airplane by 1920.

"Home Again Blues" was a popular Dixieland jazz song, though "the blues" doesn't come close to describing what many men and women experienced when returning home from the war. Post-Traumatic Stress Disorder is fairly well-known today, if not always well understood, but after World War I, "shell shock" at the incalculable horrors of war was considered a sign of weakness that veterans should "get over," leading many of the "Lost Generation" to suffer in silence. The terrible strains of World War I led to the excesses of the Roaring Twenties, including, perhaps, the rise in alcoholism during Prohibition as suffering people attempted to self-medicate with unsafe homemade alcohol.

Tin masks like the one worn by Mel Young were one of the advancements in medicine and prosthetics that came from the horrendous casualties of World War I. Many young men returned from the war missing limbs or disfigured by facial injuries. In the absence of plastic surgery, the masks replicated their pre-injury appearance and allowed them a measure of protection from the stares, rude comments, and fear of those who were unaccustomed to the brutal effects of the war.

For More Information

Flying Machine Over Zion by Anthony Martini details the earliest history of flight in Utah.

The Air Devils by Don Dwiggins recounts the feats of World War I pilots, barnstormers, and other pioneers of aviation.

Hispanics in a Mormon Zion by Jorge Iber provides an overview of the growth of the Hispanic population in Utah, both those who are members of the Church of Jesus Christ of Latter-day Saints and those who are not.

History of Kane County edited by Adonis Findlay Robinson and published by Kane County Daughters of Utah Pioneers contains a detailed history of many aspects of life in Kanab and Kane County.

ACKNOWLEDGMENTS

Thank you to everyone who helped make this book possible. Valerie, Eric, and my in-laws, the women of the Gil y Garcia family, provided valuable cultural insights, as did my husband Dan. I relied on numerous journals and newspaper articles from Kane County in the 1920s, but none were as meaningful as the family stories preserved by my grandmother, Corris Cram Brooksby. I am indebted as always to readers and critique partners who provided feedback on my writing, especially Britney, Karen, Keri, many members of the Cache Valley Chapter of the League of Utah Writers, and fellow authors Melanie Bateman, R.C. Hancock, and Chadd VanZanten (check out their awesome books!). As always, special thanks to my wonderful family for their ongoing support.

ABOUT THE AUTHOR

E.B. Wheeler attended BYU, majoring in history with an English minor, and earned graduate degrees in history and landscape architecture from Utah State University. She's the award-winning author of *The Haunting of Springett Hall,* Whitney Award finalist *Born to Treason, No Peace with the Dawn* (with Jeffery Bateman), and *Wishwood,* as well as several short stories, magazine articles, and scripts for educational software programs. She was named the 2016 Writer of the Year by the League of Utah Writers. In addition to writing, she consults about historic preservation and teaches history at USU.

You can find her online at www.ebwheeler.com

www.ingramcontent.com/pod-product-compliance
Lightning Source LLC
Chambersburg PA
CBHW071925220626
47052CB00002B/459